"I should get going," Patrick said.

Shelby turned away to open the book-drop bin beneath the window. As she raised the lid, a long, black shape slithered onto the floor and coiled in front of her. A scream tore from her throat.

Raising its head, the cottonmouth snake reared back and opened its jaws, revealing its needle, sharp fangs.

Patrick vaulted over the counter and swept Shelby into his arms. The snake struck his boot, twisting its head to drive its fangs and venom deep. Patrick knew this was no accident, but why would anyone want to harm someone as sweet as Shelby?

* * *

WITHOUT A TRACE: Will a young mother's disappearance bring a bayou town together...or tear it apart?

What Sarah Saw–Margaret Daley, January 2009
Framed!–Robin Caroll, February 2009
Cold Case Murder–Shirlee McCoy, March 2009
A Cloud of Suspicion–Patricia Davids, April 2009
Deadly Competition–Roxanne Rustand, May 2009
Her Last Chance–Terri Reed, June 2009

Books by Patricia Davids

Love Inspired Suspense

A Cloud of Suspicion

Love Inspired

His Bundle of Love
Love Thine Enemy
Prodigal Daughter
The Color of Courage
Military Daddy
A Matter of the Heart

PATRICIA DAVIDS

continues to work as a part-time nurse in the NICU while writing full-time. She enjoys researching new stories, traveling to new locations and meeting fans along the way. She and her husband of thirty-two years live in Wichita, Kansas, along with the newest addition to the household, a stray cat named Spooky. Pat always enjoys hearing from her readers. You can contact her by mail at P.O. Box 16714, Wichita, Kansas 67216, or visit her on the Web at www.patriciadavids.com.

A CLOUD OF SUSPICION

PATRICIA DAVIDS

Steeple
Hill®

Published by Steeple Hill Books™

Special thanks and acknowledgment to Patricia Davids
for her contribution to the Without a Trace miniseries.

STEEPLE HILL BOOKS

Steeple
Hill®

Recycling programs
for this product may
not exist in your area.

ISBN-13: 978-0-373-44334-5
ISBN-10:   0-373-44334-X

A CLOUD OF SUSPICION

Copyright © 2009 by Harlequin Books S.A.

www.SteepleHill.com

Printed in U.S.A.

In the day of my trouble I will call upon thee: for thou wilt answer me.

—*Psalms* 86:7

This book is dedicated with great love and deep respect to my father, Clarence. Thanks for the swing, the collie puppy, my first horse, your used car and the occasional loan. But most of all—thanks, Daddy, for the gift of your endless love.

PROLOGUE

Shelby Mason sat bolt upright in the darkness, her heart pounding in her chest. The next shrill ring of the phone dimmed her nightmare-induced panic, pulling her back into reality.

She glanced at the glowing numbers on her clock. 3:14 a.m. Who would be calling now? Who else had died?

A third ring prodded her to pick up the handset. "Hello?"

"Shelby, it's Clint Herald. Is Leah there?" His voice vibrated with anxiety.

Shelby pushed her long red hair out of her face. "Clint, do you know what time it is?"

"I know it's late, but Leah hasn't come back to pick up Sarah and she hasn't called. I'm worried sick."

Pressing a hand to her forehead, Shelby tried to make her sleep-soaked brain work better. The dregs of her fading nightmare made it hard to focus. "I haven't seen your sister since yesterday morning. Have you tried her cell phone?"

"Dozens of times. It goes straight to voice mail. She dropped Sarah off with me this evening and said she had a meeting, but it wouldn't take long. Do you have any idea where she might be or who she was seeing?"

His concern was contagious. Shelby scooted back to lean against the headboard. "No, but I'm sure there's a rational explanation. Maybe she needed some time alone. The past few days have been really rough for her."

"I thought of that, but she wouldn't leave Sarah for this long without letting me know. Something's wrong."

He was right. Leah always put her three-year-old daughter first. "Have you called the police?"

"They say they can't do anything until she's been missing for twenty-four hours."

"What? Her husband just committed suicide, and the police won't start a search for her? That's crazy."

"I told them that, but it didn't do any good. Did she seem okay when you were with her? Did you see her talking to anyone out of the ordinary?"

Shelby racked her mind. "No. She did seem preoccupied, but I assumed it was still the shock of Earl's death."

"All right," he conceded, resignation heavy in his words. "I'm sorry I bothered you."

"Don't be sorry. Call me as soon as you hear from her. I don't care what time it is. Can I do anything?"

"At this point, just pray."

"Of course."

After hanging up, Shelby swung her legs over the side of the bed. Sleep was usually impossible after the recurring nightmare she could never fully recall. Tonight, worry for Leah pushed her dream into the background.

Rubbing her hands up and down her arms, Shelby tried to convince herself that Leah was fine. It would turn out to be a simple misunderstanding. It had to be. Leah had been through so much already.

The frantic barking of a neighbor's dog abruptly shattered the stillness.

Shelby searched the cool wooden floor with her toes until she found her slippers. Sliding into them, she rose and crossed to the tall, narrow second-story window that overlooked the street outside. Pulling back the lace curtains, she pressed her forehead against the chilly glass.

The dog stopped barking. Silence blanketed the night once more.

Outside, Loomis, Louisiana, slumbered in a cold dense January mist that rose from the swamps south of town. The streetlight at the corner was only a faint white orb that did little to penetrate the darkness. Tiny pellets of sleet occasionally hit the window, melting into drizzle.

It had been years since Loomis had seen such freak winter weather. She shivered at the thought of her friend out in it. Where was Leah?

Unanswered questions crowded Shelby's mind. What if she'd been overcome with grief and done something foolish? Leah and Earl had been having problems before his death. Could there be another man? Was she with someone else?

No! Shelby dismissed the ideas as soon as they formed. Leah knew right from wrong. The love of her family and her faith were keeping her strong.

After slipping into her pale-green cotton robe, Shelby sat in the bentwood rocker in the corner of her room and turned on her reading lamp. The burst of light did nothing to dispel her worry.

Rocking back and forth, she let the creaking of the chair keep her company as she waited for Clint's call and watched the numbers on the clock tick past. Silently, she prayed for her friend.

Hours later, when the early-morning sunlight spilling through her window finally overpowered the lamp, she turned it off.

The storm had passed, but Clint hadn't called. That meant only one thing.

Leah hadn't come home.

ONE

"It's been nearly three months since Leah vanished. How can the FBI still be clueless? What's the matter with you people?" Wendy Goodwin demanded.

"Hush, Wendy." Shelby grabbed her cousin's arm. Throwing an apologetic look at FBI agent Jodie Gilmore, Shelby asked, "Nothing new at all? I thought when I saw you back in town there might be a new lead."

Jodie's eyes held sympathy and understanding. "I'm only here because the home office received a phone tip we thought worth checking into. It didn't pan out. We haven't had a solid new lead since the discovery of Leah's shoe in February at that abandoned house in the swamp."

The slipper hadn't led them to Leah. Instead, it led investigators to uncover and solve a twenty-five-year-old triple murder. One of the victims had been Jodie's mother. Another Loomis woman who had vanished without a trace.

If anyone in the bureau would keep looking for answers, it would be Jodie.

Shelby nodded her thanks. She came by the sheriff's office at least three times a week to check on her friend's case. As the months passed with no new information, the FBI's Missing Persons task force had gone back to New Orleans.

When Shelby saw Jodie today, her hopes had risen, but once again she faced bitter disappointment.

Soon they would call off the search and give Leah up for dead.

"I think it's just criminal you people aren't doing more." Wendy raised her voice in a parting shot.

Shelby dragged her cousin out the door. Her sentiments might be the same as Wendy's, but she could never voice them the way her outspoken cousin did.

Once outside the sheriff's office, Shelby released Wendy. "I want Leah to be found as much as you do, but insulting the people looking for her isn't going to help."

Wendy crossed her arms and shivered, although the morning was warm with late March sunshine and rising humidity. "It's just so frightening. How does someone we know vanish? This kind of thing happens only in movies."

"It happens in real life, too, Wendy."

"It doesn't happen to your friend. To someone who attends the same church. To someone who brings her daughter to our library for Story Hour."

Shelby drew Wendy close in a comforting hug. "I know. I'm frustrated, too, but the sheriff's office insists they are doing all they can."

"Do you think she's dead?" Wendy whispered.

Pulling back, Shelby gazed into her cousin's worry-filled blue eyes. With one hand she smoothed back a lock of Wendy's blond hair. "I can't think that way. I have to believe she's alive."

Please, Lord, let it be true for little Sarah's sake.

Wendy rubbed the back of her neck as she admitted, "After the other murders, it's hard to hold on to hope."

"That's why we have to put our faith in God. He's watching over Leah."

Wendy cast a glance around. "I know you're right, but you can't deny this is a scary time. I get up a dozen times at night to make sure the doors and windows are locked. I don't go out after dark. I don't let the kids play outside alone. I look twice at everyone I know and I think, could it be them?"

Depression dragged at Shelby's spirits. "I know. I feel the same way."

"The whole town is on edge. I thought for sure when Vera Peel was arrested two weeks ago for the old murders that she was the killer. Some people are still insisting she is. Dylan Renault and Angelina Loring were both struck over the head and shot in the back, just like the skeletons that were found in that old cellar."

"Vera Peel confessed to killing her husband, Jodie's mother and that poor woman in the gazebo twenty-five years ago, but she has an alibi for the time of Dylan's murder. Besides, Leah's husband wasn't shot in the back."

"But Earl *was* shot, and it wasn't suicide. Some people are saying—"

"I know they're saying Leah killed Earl for the insurance money, that she panicked and skipped town, that she ran off with some unknown lover. None of it is true."

None of it makes sense. Lord, we need Your help. Please keep Leah safe and bring her home to us.

Releasing her cousin, Shelby started toward the crosswalk at the corner of Church Street and Main. Their destination was the restaurant inside the Loomis Hotel. Coffee made with chicory and scalded milk and the mouth-watering beignets at the posh Café Au Lait were a Monday-morning custom the women had enjoyed for the past two years.

Shelby, Wendy and Leah had first chosen the high-class setting to celebrate Shelby's appointment as head librarian at the Loomis Public Library. The women had been starting their work week in the same way ever since.

When Shelby and Leah's high-school friend, Jocelyn Gold, returned to Loomis to open up a practice as a child psychologist, they were quick to include her in their tradition. They'd shared some great times and plenty of laughter together.

Knowing Leah wouldn't be joining them put a damper on what used to be a lighthearted gathering, but sticking to the ritual had become a means of keeping each other's spirits up.

"How can y'all be so sure Leah isn't guilty?" Wendy asked. "We never know what another person is capable of doing."

Shelby didn't hesitate. "Leah wouldn't abandon Sarah. That little girl is everything to her."

"You're right. I'm going crazy with all the uncertainty. Leah couldn't ask for a better friend than you, Shelby."

"I wish that were true. If I'd been a better friend, she might have confided in me. I knew something was bothering her, I just didn't think it was any of my business."

They were almost at their destination when Shelby noticed a motorcycle occupying a parking space in front of the hotel. The custom chrome-and-black machine crouched in the line of sedans and SUVs, looking like a panther among a herd of milk cows.

The leather studded saddlebags over the rear tire conjured up images of life on the road, escape, excitement, daring. All the things Shelby read about in the books at the city library where she worked but had never experienced for herself.

Looking over her shoulder as she pulled open the café door, she couldn't help the wistful tone in her voice as she stepped inside. "I wonder who that belongs to."

"It's mine."

At the sound of a man's low rumbling voice, a feeling of

electricity raced over her nerve endings. Her head whipped around, and Shelby found herself staring at the zipper of a black leather jacket decorated with the same silver studs as the saddlebags.

Looking higher, she met the owner's dark hooded gaze and recognition hit her like a kick to the stomach.

Patrick Rivers was back in Loomis.

It took Patrick a few seconds to place the petite woman with a cascade of thick red hair swirling about her shoulders. Her light-brown eyes widened and color flooded her cheeks in two perfect circles of berry-bright skin.

Only one woman he remembered in Loomis could blush so sweetly. Chunky, shy Shelby Mason had bloomed into a true Southern rose.

A wry smile pulled at the corner of his mouth. The word *chunky* no longer applied. Her soft lilac dress with tiny white polka dots accented her feminine curves to perfection.

Her quick indrawn breath and the backward step she took confirmed what he already suspected. She recognized him, too.

"Miss Mason, isn't it?" he asked.

Irritation swept over him at how easily the Louisiana drawl returned to his voice. He'd worked hard to remove any reminders of Loomis from his life, including his accent.

Her hand went to her throat. A flutter of nervousness that she couldn't hide made her fingers tremble. She regarded him with suspicion. Like everyone else in the gloomy city. Anger rose like bitter bile in his mouth.

There was no place like home—home sweet home.

To her credit, Shelby quickly regained her composure. "Mr. Rivers. I heard that your stepfather had passed away. Please accept my condolences."

The pure charm of her lilting voice took him straight back in time. Back ten years to the days when the local college girls had flirted outrageously with a poor boy from the wrong side of the tracks because he could throw a football better than anyone in St. Tammany Parish.

Back to the night one spoiled, vain debutante ruined his life.

It didn't matter that he had been innocent of the crime, that the charges had been dropped. Coral Travis had accused him of rape. The stigma stuck to him like the odor of rotting vegetation permeated the black mud of the bayou.

He had tried to face down the rumors, the looks, the mistrust, but in the end leaving had been his only option.

Gritting his teeth against the pain of those memories, he gave Shelby a brief nod. "Thanks, but Dan and I weren't that close."

Did he imagine sympathy filled her eyes before she looked down? He wanted to reach out and lift her chin to be sure. Kindness from anyone in Loomis was a rare thing.

Her long lashes fluttered up as she met his gaze again. The morning sunlight brought out flecks of green in her eyes that he'd never noticed before. Beneath the overpowering aromas of coffee and pastry he caught a subtle hint of her fresh flowery fragrance.

When had the self-effacing little librarian grown to be such a beauty?

Realizing he was blocking the doorway, he stepped aside and allowed her to enter. To his surprise, she didn't rush past him the way her companion did, but paused at his side.

A half smile trembled on her lips. She looked adorably uncertain of the correct way to address an accused rapist. Finally, she managed to ask, "Will you be staying in Loomis long?"

A sharp gasp made him look beyond Shelby to see the architect of his disgrace staring at him in wide-eyed shock.

Coldness settled in his chest and spread through his body. This was exactly the scene he'd dreaded from the minute he knew he was coming back to Loomis.

Of course, it had to happen in front of dozens of witnesses.

Only years of practice at keeping his emotions hidden prevented him from bolting out the door. His indifference might be a veneer, but time and pain had made it thick. He didn't move so much as a muscle.

Coral Travis hadn't changed much in the intervening years. She was still a beautiful woman. Her hair, a lighter shade of blond now, was styled loose about her shoulders. Dressed in a white ensemble, she clung to the arm of a tall handsome blond man in a tailored gray suit. They made a striking couple. Behind them stood five more men in business attire.

Staring at Coral, Patrick saw the shock in her eyes quickly change to fury, then a hard look of calculation develop in their depths. Her gaze shifted to Shelby without softening.

He glanced around the café with its rich dark paneling. High-backed booths edged the room and a dozen tables covered with snowy white cloths filled the rest of the space. Every table was occupied. The hum of conversations stilled. People began staring and whispering to each other.

He recognized some of the faces, all older, all judgmental.

Don't give them the satisfaction of seeing you care.

Deliberately raising his voice, he focused on Shelby. "It's been a pleasure seeing you again, Miss Mason. Let's get together and talk about old times. Remember the football championship?" Bitterness burned like acid on his tongue as he glared at Coral. "More than one game was played that night." He nodded to Shelby. "I'll be in town a week or two unless the sheriff runs me out sooner. Is Bradford Reed still sheriff around here?"

"Yes, he is." Shelby's eyes darted to Coral and back to him. He read her confusion and discomfort. Suddenly, he wished he hadn't used her to take a jab at Coral.

"Things haven't changed much here, have they?" he stated bitterly and loud enough to be overheard by everyone.

Before she could answer, Patrick walked out the door and let it slam shut behind him.

Shelby stood aside as Coral, pausing only to shoot a look of malice at Shelby, left the building followed by her fiancé, Wendell Bixby, and the other members of Wendell's election committee. As the door closed behind them, Shelby stepped to the window and watched them quickly cross the street.

Patrick strolled to his bike, looking like he didn't have a care in the world.

Shelby wasn't exactly sure *what* had just happened. Somehow, she'd found herself in the cross fire between Patrick and Coral. Talk about uncomfortable.

But then, nothing between Shelby and Coral had been comfortable since the night of Coral's alleged rape. Shelby didn't know the whole story, but she knew enough to wonder if Coral had lied. Only—why would she?

Shelby watched Patrick settle astride his motorcycle and pull it upright. She wanted to believe he had been innocent of the charges Coral leveled against him, but only the two of them knew for certain what happened that night.

Studying Patrick, Shelby decided that he had changed a good deal since college. His hair was still a thick sable brown, but he wore it shorter now and there was a touch of gray at his temples. Fine crow's-feet fanned out from the corners of his dark-as-molasses eyes giving him a world-weary look.

Tilting her head slightly, she decided it was more of a world-*wary* look.

Drawing a pair of aviator sunglasses from his breast pocket, he slipped them on. Shelby's heart skipped a beat—or two. His magnetic, bad-boy aura hadn't dimmed a bit over the years. If anything, he was more attractive than ever.

Dressed in a leather jacket, tight faded jeans and black boots, he looked like he had ridden straight off a movie set. He looked like trouble waiting to pounce on an unsuspecting town.

She jumped a fraction when the bike roared to life. After revving the engine, he backed out of the parking space and rode away. Only then did she come out of her mental fog.

"On the contrary, Mr. Rivers," she muttered softly. "Things have changed a great deal in Loomis in the past few months, and none of it for the better."

"Who is he, and how do you know a hunk like that?" Wendy demanded at her elbow, her voice brimming with awe.

Taking in the number of people staring at them, Shelby steered Wendy to the nearest booth where Jocelyn was already waiting for them and watching the exchange with interest.

Jocelyn's recent wedding to FBI agent Sam Pierce had been a bright spot in the otherwise frightening events of the year. Dressed in a beige suit jacket with dark-brown piping, Jocelyn radiated professional confidence and a quiet happiness Shelby envied.

Wendy scooted into the booth beside her. Wearing a purple, flowing print skirt and lacy camisole top under a crocheted multicolored shrug, Wendy radiated…Wendy.

"Yes, Shelby," Jocelyn added with a curious smile. "Do tell us who that was."

Shelby slid across the red vinyl bench opposite Jocelyn and Wendy and glanced at her cousin. "You don't remember Patrick Rivers?"

Wendy tipped her head. "Should I?"

"You were two years behind me in school, so maybe you didn't know about him."

A slight frown marred Jocelyn's forehead. "I don't remember him, either."

"You had already moved away," Shelby explained. "He was a junior when I was a freshman at Loomis College. He was the football captain and quarterback. NFL scouts were lining up around the block to watch him."

Wendy's eyes widened with sudden shock. "He's the guy that raped Coral Travis."

Casting Wendy a quelling glance, Shelby leaned forward and spoke quietly. "The charges were dismissed due to lack of evidence."

"Which means he got away with it," Wendy declared. "No wonder she looked like she'd seen a ghost. Do you think there's a connection between Leah's disappearance, the murders and his sudden return?"

Was there?

Shaking her head, Shelby lifted a laminated menu from the metal holder at the end of the table. "I don't see how. I'm sure it's just a coincidence that he's here now. His stepfather died a few weeks ago."

Wendy looked unconvinced. "He could be back to get his revenge. Did y'all see the cold way he looked at Coral? First a murderer loose in town and now a rapist. I'm telling you, Shelby Sue, I have no idea what this town is coming to. I feel like locking myself in the house and swallowing the key."

Reaching across the table, Shelby covered Wendy's hand with her own. "Then who would help me run the library, Wendy Jean?"

"No one. I'd lock you in the house with me."

Jocelyn slipped her arm around Wendy's shoulders. "We should all be careful, but we can't hide from life. Now more than ever, the people of this town—particularly the children—need normalcy."

"And caution…and mace," Wendy declared. "I'm getting y'all cans of pepper spray the minute we leave here."

Shelby smiled. "You know what a klutz I am. I'd end up spraying myself in the face."

"Don't make light of this. I've lost one friend already. I don't want to lose you, too. Maybe if Leah had had something to defend herself with…" Wendy's voice trailed off.

"I think about that, too," Jocelyn added quietly.

In the sudden stillness, Shelby knew they were all thinking the same thing. Three people they knew had been murdered. Leah was most likely dead, her body disposed of somewhere in the trackless miles of swamp.

A killer was still on the loose in their town. How soon would he or she kill again? Who would be the next victim?

TWO

The house wasn't much to look at.

Patrick turned off his bike and sat staring at the sky-blue cottage situated near the outskirts of Loomis. His childhood home, such as it was, hadn't seen a new coat of paint in years. Perhaps not since he'd left a decade ago.

The steamy Louisiana humidity wasn't kind to bare wood. He'd be lucky if there wasn't rot in the steps leading up to the narrow front porch.

He put down the kickstand and swung his leg over the seat. Standing upright, he stretched a few residual kinks out of his back. Los Angeles was a long, long way from Loomis.

He'd spent last night at the hotel because his stepfather's attorney's office had been closed when Patrick rolled into town. In a way, the delay had been good. He certainly hadn't wanted to revisit his personal ghosts at night. It was hard enough in the light of day.

The only bright spot in the whole trip had been seeing Shelby Mason again. It surprised him how attractive he found her. He'd made a habit of avoiding serious involvements with women, and with good reason.

What would it be like to be an ordinary man in Loomis?

To speak to a pretty woman without worrying about the stares and whispers?

Forget it. It's not going to happen. If I needed proof, I got it this morning.

He was here to settle his stepfather's estate, nothing more. He couldn't change the past. All he could hope for was to profit from the present.

Avoiding the inevitable for a few minutes longer, he walked around the side of the house.

His boots crunched on the crushed oyster shell path that led past the detached garage to the backyard. He noticed the garage was in better shape than the house. The outside of the building was covered with new vinyl siding.

His stepdad had always enjoyed working in his shop, tinkering on his car or his lawnmower. A love of engines was about the only thing the two of them had in common.

Walking to the rear of the house, Patrick stopped at the sight that met him. The grass was knee-high. Honeysuckle vines and kudzu ran rampant over the chain link fence at the back of the property. An air of neglect hung over everything.

Looking at the single live oak tree in the center of the yard, he noticed a piece of weathered rope dangling from a branch. It was all that was left of the tire swing he'd used to hone his throwing arm.

He closed his eyes and breathed in. The coy, sweet fragrance of the flowering honeysuckle took him back to his childhood.

He could almost hear his mother's voice calling him in to supper from a game of hide-and-seek with the neighborhood kids. How many summer evenings had he spent catching fireflies in this yard? How many nights had he camped out here under a makeshift tent with his best buddy, Wyatt? How many times had Wyatt's family taken him along on their fishing trips to their cabin in the woods?

Sadness crept over Patrick. How could so much heartache and pain reside in the same place where he had known such happiness as a kid?

"I'm surprised you came back."

Patrick's eyes flew open at the sound of a man's voice. Turning around, he found himself staring at his friend, Wyatt, grown up now and watching with dark eyes narrowed in displeasure from the back porch of the house next door.

Patrick swallowed the bitterness rising to the back of his throat. "Hello, Wyatt. It's nice to see you, too."

Wyatt Tibbs dropped his gaze. His lips pressed into a thin line, then he said, "Sorry about your stepdad."

"Thanks." Patrick motioned toward the well-kept white bungalow with blue shutters where Wyatt stood. "How are your folks?"

Making small talk was easier than tackling the big issue that lay between the two men. At least it was something.

"They moved to Arizona a few years back. I own the place now. Are you staying long?" Wyatt's tone made it plain that Patrick wasn't welcome.

Resentment simmered as Patrick stared at his former friend. "I don't know. Maybe I'll move back here for good," he suggested with thick sarcasm.

A woman's voice called out from inside Wyatt's house. "Honey, breakfast is ready."

Wyatt glanced from Patrick to his own door and then back. "Staying isn't a good idea."

"I didn't do it, you know." Patrick had no idea why he felt compelled to defend himself again after ten years. No one had believed him then. Nothing had changed.

Wyatt stared at him for a long moment. "Like I said, staying isn't a good idea." He walked into his house, letting the screen door slam behind him.

Annoyed with himself for caring so much, Patrick blew out a breath between pursed lips and headed back to the front of the house. He needed to get rid of this part of his life. For good.

Climbing the steps, he pulled out the key his stepfather's attorney had given him a short time ago and unlocked the front door.

The clinking of silverware against china and the murmur of voices surrounded Shelby as she waited on everyone to finish their French donuts. After licking a dusting of powdered sugar from her lips, she took a sip of her second cup of coffee.

Across the table, Wendy began folding and unfolding her napkin. "I heard they might cancel the Mother of the Year Pageant."

Jocelyn nodded. "Ava Renault mentioned that the planning committee has seriously been considering it."

Wendy crossed her arms and rubbed her hands up and down her sleeves. "After Jillian Morrison got a note telling her to withdraw or end up dead and then poor Nancy Bailey had bleach thrown in her face—well, it's a wonder anyone is willing to be a contestant. I certainly don't want to be nominated."

"What do you think about canceling it?" Shelby asked Jocelyn.

"On one hand, I see it as an act of respect for Angelina and Dylan's deaths and Leah's disappearance, but on the other hand, it means the town is giving in to fear. I hope they don't cancel it."

Looking from Shelby to Jocelyn, Wendy said, "I know y'all were close friends with Leah in high school so you know her better than almost anyone. Do you think there's any truth to the rumor that Dylan Renault is Sarah's father?"

Shelby bit her lip. It wasn't possible, was it? Yet Dylan Renault's dying words had been, "Sarah's father." Words whispered in the ear of FBI agent Sam Pierce, Jocelyn's husband.

No one was sure what Dylan meant by them but there was plenty of speculation.

Sensing Shelby's hesitation, Wendy arched her eyebrows. "You know something you aren't telling us."

Shaking her head in denial, Shelby said, "I only know that Leah worked as Dylan's secretary before she married Earl and that Dylan made her uncomfortable with his attention. She stopped working for him pretty abruptly after that company Christmas party four years ago."

Jocelyn tipped her head slightly as she stared at Shelby. "Did something happen at that party?"

A shiver ran over Shelby's skin. She didn't like thinking about that night. She had attended at Leah's insistence but had become so ill she later fainted. The whole night was nothing but a weird blur.

Afterward, Shelby began having nightmares—the same dream over and over again. A disembodied face looking down at her, laughing at her.

Pushing aside thoughts of her haunting dream, Shelby nodded. "Something happened that upset Leah a great deal, but she never talked about it."

Jocelyn pushed aside her plate and folded her hands on the table. "Have you told Sam about this?"

"No."

"I think you should. The FBI has been searching for a connection between Leah's disappearance and Dylan's murder."

"I wish I could remember more. I got sick at the party and Leah did, too. I have this dream about that night, but I'm not sure what it means."

"I might be able to help," Jocelyn suggested.

Embarrassed, Shelby shook her head. "It's just a dream."

Wendy's eyes narrowed as she leaned forward. "Who else was there? Maybe they know something."

"A lot of people were there, but most of them were friends of Dylan's. Not exactly my social circle."

Shelby glanced toward the door. A long-forgotten face swam into focus. "Wendell Bixby was there. He worked for Renault Corporation back then. I could talk to him and see if he remembers anything odd about Dylan or Leah's behavior."

"Such idle gossip benefits no one, Miss Mason." The hard, cultured voice of Charla Renault caught Shelby unaware. She hadn't heard Charla's electric wheelchair coming up behind her.

The scent of White Shoulders perfume mingled with the coffee and cinnamon in the air. Shelby turned in her seat to face the mother of the most recent murder victim in Loomis.

Charla's dark eyes glittered with cold anger. "*My son* was never interested in someone as common as Leah Farley."

Shelby wished she hadn't been caught in the act of talking about the woman's son. She wanted to defend Leah, but Charla had a way of making Shelby, and most of Loomis, feel small and insignificant. "I beg your pardon, Mrs. Renault."

The man who worked as Charla's driver and servant rose from the booth behind Shelby. He settled his hat on his thick gray hair and ran a hand down the front of his impeccably pressed black chauffeur's jacket. Apparently, he had been waiting for Charla to finish her breakfast, because he nodded to her and asked, "Shall I bring the car around, madame?"

"Yes." She dismissed him with a wave. Although Charla Renault maintained a regal air, neither wealth nor social position had spared the matriarch of the Renault family her share of pain. Confined to a wheelchair after the car accident that claimed her husband's life, Charla still ruled the family with an iron fist in a kid glove.

Dressed today in a pink twinset with a simple choker of small pink pearls at her throat, Charla looked the epitome of Southern class, but the death of her only son had been a blow from which many wondered if she would ever recover. Now she had only her daughter, Ava, to carry on the family traditions and businesses.

The word that Ava had recently become engaged to Max Pershing, son of Charla's archrival and longtime social enemy, Lenore Pershing, was a prime bit of news making the rounds. The two families had been feuding for ages. Shelby could only pray that Max and Ava's love would put an end to their family's long-standing grudge once and for all.

Jocelyn spoke up. "It's nice to see you out and about, Mrs. Renault."

"Thank you." Charla inclined her head, ever so slightly. As always, not a single dark hair dared slip out of place or show the smallest touch of gray. In her lap, her Jack Russell terrier, Rhett, growled low in his throat.

Charla laid a hand on the dog's head to silence him and focused her gaze on Shelby. "I was just on my way to see you, Miss Mason."

Taken aback, Shelby stuttered, "You…you wanted to see me?"

"Yes. Since my son's untimely passing, I have been pondering how best to honor his memory in the community that he served with such devotion and dignity. I am considering making a sizable donation to the city library in his name."

Shelby was sure she must look like a stunned pelican with her gaping mouth. "Mrs. Renault, I'm not sure what to say."

Charla held up one hand, silencing Shelby as easily as she had the dog. "I'm also considering funding a scholarship in his name at the college. I would, of course, need assurance that the institution I choose will provide a lasting memorial that is befitting of the Renault name. I'd like to see a proposal from the library board on such a memorial by the end of next week."

"Next week?" Shelby blinked hard.

"The dean at Loomis College assured me that a week would be sufficient time to present a plan. If you don't feel up to the task, Miss Mason, I must wonder if you're the right person to be in charge of our venerable and historic library."

As the youngest head librarian ever employed by the city, Shelby had faced her share of detractors when she applied for the job, but she knew the library was prospering under her guidance.

Still, the city never had enough money in the budget to cover all the expenses and upkeep the "venerable and historic" building needed. *Old* and *needy* would be a more apt description of the place.

The chance to gain a sizable donation from the Renault family was a windfall that couldn't be ignored.

"We have a general meeting of the board a week from Thursday, Mrs. Renault. You're welcome to attend. I'm sure I can work up a proposal that will satisfy both your needs and the needs of our community."

"Good, Miss Mason. However, should it come to my attention that you're continuing to engage in baseless gossip about my son…well, I'm sure y'all can see how that would influence my decision."

"Of course, Mrs. Renault." It meant Charla would take her money elsewhere without batting an eye.

With another slight tilt of her head, Charla maneuvered her chair down the aisle toward the door, where the owner of Café Au Lait hurried to hold it open for her.

Wendy blew out a deep breath. "Her son's death hasn't changed her a bit."

"Why do you say that?" Jocelyn asked.

"Because she still enjoys pitting people against each other. Shelby, you know the college will be crawling all over themselves to gain the old gal's favor. They'll cater to her every whim."

"I'll simply have to convince her that we can provide a better memorial than they can."

Jocelyn gathered up her purse. "How are you going to do that?"

Shaking her head, Shelby admitted, "I have absolutely no idea."

Wendy wrapped the last beignet in a napkin and stuffed it in her handbag. "Did you like him? I don't mean to speak ill of the dead, but was Dylan Renault the kind of man who deserved to have a scholarship or a new library wing named after him?"

Shelby smiled sadly. "I didn't like him, but I can't blame his mother for wanting to see that her son's name is treated with respect. We know it doesn't matter if a dozen libraries are named after him. God is the final judge of us all. Only He knows the soul of Dylan Renault."

Jocelyn laid a tip on the table. "Are you going to talk to Sam about the Christmas party?"

Shelby hesitated. She didn't actually know anything. It was more of a feeling. Still, Jocelyn and Ava were close friends. What if it got back to Charla that Shelby was talking about Dylan again?

The college will be rubbing their hands with glee over their new donation, that's what.

"I'll call Sam if I remember something concrete. Otherwise, don't say anything about it. I feel silly for mentioning it."

After paying the check, the women left the café. With a round of quick hugs and promises to meet again next week, they parted ways. Jocelyn left for her office, while Shelby and Wendy walked toward the library. Shelby found herself checking the street for Patrick's motorcycle, but to no avail.

She had been stunned to see him again after all this time, but she was honest enough to admit that surprise had been only part of her pulse-pounding reaction to the man. He was dangerously attractive, even more so now than when she had last seen him.

What she found truly disturbing was how much she wanted to see him again.

After crossing Main Street, Shelby and Wendy cut through the park on a paved path that led toward the city library. The smell of damp, newly cut grass hung in the air and mixed with the scent of flowers and blooming shrubs. The two women hurried past the small white gazebo standing alone at the center of the park.

At first glance, the lattice-covered structure looked picture-perfect in the setting, but on closer inspection one could see the paint was peeling and some of the slats were broken.

People who lived in Loomis knew that a woman had been murdered inside the gazebo twenty-five years ago. The death of that young mother was the reason Loomis started their annual Mother's Day Festival with their Mother of the Year Pageant.

The pageant had grown from humble beginnings into the town's biggest event with prize money worth thousands of dollars going to the mother who was chosen as the winner. Over the years, the money, gifts and prestige of winning had sparked some serious rivalries and even resulted in foul play among the women vying for Loomis's most coveted title.

The mystery of the woman's death had been solved when

Vera Peel confessed to killing the amateur photographer because she had been taking pictures of the bayou the day Vera killed her husband and his lover there.

Even knowing how and why the woman had died hadn't altered people's perception of the gazebo. Only newcomers or visitors used it. The locals continued to give it a wide berth.

Suddenly a creaking, scuffling sound made Shelby and Wendy spin around in fright. A dark figure sat on the floor inside the structure.

It took a heart-stopping second for Shelby to recognize Chuck Peters, the town drunk who panhandled and did odd jobs around the city.

"I didn't see nothing. I didn't," he muttered, and lurched to his feet.

Shelby sucked in several calming breaths, then took a step toward him. "Mr. Peters, you frightened us."

He swayed slightly as he peered at them through his thick, black-rimmed glasses. During one of his sober spells, Chuck had worked briefly for Shelby's father at his wood-working shop. After her father passed away, Chuck started doing odd jobs for the reclusive Vera Peel. With his bene-factress now in jail for murder, Shelby had to wonder how he was managing.

Wendy tugged at Shelby's arm. "Come on. Let's go."

"Mr. Peters, do you need me to call Reverend Harmon for you?"

His eyes widened with fear. "No! Don't call him. Don't tell anyone you saw me here. Don't tell. Swear you won't tell!"

Hoping to reassure him, Shelby added quickly, "But Reverend Harmon can get you a hot meal and a place to stay."

"No, I like this place. I can see who's coming." His eyes darted around like frightened birds seeking a way out of a cage.

"You can't stay here. The police won't let you," she said gently.

It was obvious that he was more disturbed than usual. He ran his hands through his greasy, thinning red hair. "Don't tell 'em I'm here. I didn't see nothing that night. You can't say I did."

"What night, Mr. Peters?"

"Can't say. Don't know. Didn't see nothing that night."

Wendy pulled harder on Shelby's arm. "Let's go. You can't help him if he doesn't want it."

Shelby allowed herself to be led away. "I'm going to call Reverend Harmon anyway. He's dealt with Chuck in the past."

"That's a good idea. Maybe he can get the old loony back into the mental hospital where he belongs."

"Wendy!" Shelby glanced back, but Chuck didn't seem to be paying attention to them. He was making his way out of the gazebo with unsteady steps.

Beyond him, Shelby noticed another figure lurking in the shadows near the path. The man turned away abruptly before Shelby could see who it was.

"I'm only suggesting that Reverend Harmon can supply him with the professional help he needs." Wendy defended her suggestion. "Let's get out of this park. It's creepy in here."

Shelby had to agree, although she had always enjoyed the peace and quiet of the secluded place. Now, the tall live oak trees hung with Spanish moss seemed vaguely threatening. The thick azalea bushes laden with blooms seemed to offer hiding places for danger along with their beauty.

Like nearly everyone in Loomis, she found the fear of an unknown killer in their midst had changed her perspective of her hometown.

* * *

Mustiness assailed Patrick as he stepped into the front parlor. Little had changed in the years that he had been gone. The same faded area rug still covered the center of the hardwood floor. The same beige sofa sat in front of the small bay window. Dirt darkened the armrests of the matching chair across the room.

There was an empty coffee mug and stain rings on the small table beside the chair. He could picture his stepdad sitting there, staring out the window at the town that shunned him for raising a monster.

Patrick shook off the vision. For some odd reason his stepfather had stipulated in his will that if Patrick came back and settled the estate in person, it would all go to him. He didn't know why. Maybe the old man wasn't quite right in the head toward the end.

Patrick had almost refused. But the chance to gain enough to help him secure his future overrode his reluctance. Nothing else would have brought him back to Loomis.

He had a week or two to go through the place and get the house ready to go on the market. After that, he didn't have to hang around to make sure someone actually bought it. His father's attorney had been clear on that issue. All Patrick had to do was go through the belongings in the house and see to the repairs.

Looking around, Patrick began to feel a little more hopeful. The place wasn't a total ruin. With a little paint and elbow grease he should be able to sell it. How ironic would it be if his stepfather had actually handed him the means to make his dreams come true?

Before today, Patrick figured it would take him another two years of scrimping and saving to buy into a partnership at the custom bike shop where he worked. His plan was to become part owner and eventually sole proprietor of Wolfwind Cycles.

Bikes were his life. His only love. A man could count on a good machine.

If he could make enough from the sale of this place, he could push his agenda forward by several years.

Walking around the living room, Patrick tried to take a quick inventory but found himself touching things and thinking about them. His mother had loved the painting of the old barn over the fireplace. He picked up the small pewter unicorn from the mantel. He had given it to her for Christmas the year before she died.

Closing his eyes, he recalled the feel of her hugs, the scent of her perfume, the happiness in her laughter. He searched for similar memories of his stepfather but couldn't find them.

All he could hear was his stepfather's angry voice raised in accusations. All he could see was the disappointment and repugnance etched on the face of the only father Patrick had ever known.

Opening his eyes, Patrick sighed. This wasn't going to be as easy as he had hoped. Folding his fingers around the trinket, he shoved it deep in his pockets and rocked back on his heels.

There was a stack of books on the table beside his stepfather's chair. Picking up the top book, Patrick saw it was a murder mystery by a popular new writer. He opened the cover. The book had been checked out of the Loomis library three months before.

Great. I've got overdue fines to pay.

He snapped the book shut and returned it to the top of the stack.

Someone, most likely the attorney, had gathered together a pile of mail and left it on the seat of the chair. Picking it up,

Patrick sat and began to sort through it. Most of it was junk mail and old newspapers, but he did find a few bills he would have to take care of.

When he came across a late notice from the library, he read the note with special interest. It was signed by Shelby Mason.

Shelby, with the gorgeous red hair and roses in her cheeks. So she had moved from working at the college library to working at the city library. Why hadn't she left this miserable town behind?

She'd been a sweet kid. He had wanted to ask her about her life this morning at the café, but he had left instead when he saw the number of cold stares leveled in his direction.

He'd cut short the conversation as much for her sake as for his. The gossip machine in Loomis could grind her up and spit her out in no time just for passing the time of day with him.

He tossed the letter aside with a weary shake of his head. It seemed he still had a need to protect the underdog.

What made him think Shelby Mason needed protection? In Loomis, *he* was the underdog. A cur no one would speak up for.

He rose and wandered through the kitchen and down the hall that led to the back of the house. His old bedroom was the first door on the right.

Stepping inside, he wasn't surprised to find it stripped bare. His football trophies, his track ribbons, his posters of *Easy Rider,* Santana and Jennifer Lopez were all gone. His stepfather had gotten rid of every trace of him. Only the blue drapes remained to remind Patrick of the way the room once looked. He pulled the door shut.

The next room down the hall was his father's bedroom. Easing the door open, Patrick looked in. The bed was neatly made. There were a few clothes scattered around, but nothing of his mother's.

He frowned when he saw the empty bookcases lining two walls. Had his father gotten rid of his mother's books?

Diana Rivers had been an English teacher with a true love of literature and history and a passion for collecting old books. Some of Patrick's fondest memories were of the two of them traveling to estate sales, rummage sales, even auctions looking for unusual books on the state's history or first editions of her favorite authors.

Once, at a garage sale in Covington she paid a dollar for a first edition of a Mark Twain novel and had spoken of it gleefully for months afterwards.

A lumber mill worker like his father and his grandfather before him, Ben Rivers had put up with his wife's odd obsession, but he never understood why words were so important to her.

Patrick closed the bedroom door and turned to the last small room at the end of the hall. It had been his mother's sewing room. When he pushed open the door, he found himself confronted with a room stacked full of packing boxes.

Lifting the lid off the nearest one, he found it contained some of his mother's clothes. A second box held more of the same, but he relaxed when he opened the third box. In it were dozens of his mother's books.

Sinking onto the dusty floor, Patrick drew out a novel bound with thick red leather and embossed with gold lettering. He breathed in the scent of the old paper and truly smiled for the first time since he had crossed the Louisiana state line.

Shelby's day passed in a busy blur at the city library. After the weekend there were always plenty of books in the drive-up return book bin to be checked in, reshelved or mended. A rush of customers in the early afternoon kept her busy and left her little time to think about the type of memorial program she could develop for Mrs. Renault.

As busy as she was, she still found herself thinking about Patrick Rivers and the odd way he had smiled at her.

She'd had such a crush on him in college. Of course, he had barely noticed her.

As the captain of a winning football team he'd had his pick of girls, but he'd been more than a jock. He'd spent plenty of late nights studying at the campus library. Sometimes, when he stayed until she had to lock up, he would walk her to her dorm. It made her feel so special.

Looking back, her infatuation seemed silly now. Her dorm had been on the way to his place. He hadn't really been walking her home. He'd just been walking in the same direction and being kind. It had been his kindness that made the accusations about him so hard to believe.

Shelby recalled the night vividly. Patrick had just led their team to a regional championship. Most of the campus had turned out to celebrate the big win with a bonfire in a secluded part of the bayou.

Shelby had watched the merrymakers with a touch of envy. It wasn't that she wanted to drink or party, she just wanted Patrick to notice her.

He didn't, of course, because she stayed in the background, a shy mouse of a girl that no one noticed. Not like Coral Travis. Everyone noticed her.

Standing by herself in the shadows that night, Shelby overheard a disturbing conversation. She recognized Coral's voice telling someone that she was going home with Patrick, whether he knew it or not. He was her ticket out of Loomis.

Before Shelby could retreat, Coral had come out of a stand of small trees and spied her.

Shelby could still hear the mocking tone of Coral's voice.

"What are you doing here? Hoping some guy will get drunk enough to ask you out?"

From some unknown source of strength, Shelby managed to reply, "Patrick deserves better than you."

Coral only laughed and said, "Get out of the sandbox, chubby, this is where the big kids play."

Mortified, Shelby watched as Coral sauntered off and insinuated herself next to Patrick. The two of them left together less than half an hour later. Shelby took her bruised ego and wounded heart home where she indulged in a good cry.

The next day the news of Patrick's arrest for rape spread across the campus like wildfire. Nearly everyone believed it was true.

Would it have made a difference if I'd spoken up and told the police what Coral said? But what reason would Coral have had to lie about such a serious charge?

The same questions had haunted Shelby for weeks afterward. When Patrick left town, she thought the answers didn't matter anymore. Until now.

A patron approached Shelby for help finding a book. Pulling her mind out of the past, she dismissed Patrick Rivers from her thoughts and got back to work.

When five o'clock rolled around, Shelby and Wendy closed up and walked to their cars in the parking lot behind the building. The lot, shared with the town hall, the library and several other businesses, was quickly emptying as people headed home.

Shelby caught sight of Chuck Peters standing at the street corner checking a pay phone for loose coins. She knew a moment of guilt. She hadn't found time to call Reverend Harmon.

Chuck glanced in her direction. He spun around and hurried away, casting frightened glances over his shoulder.

"Shelby, look," Wendy said, drawing her attention away from the odd behavior of the little man.

Following Wendy's gaze, Shelby saw Coral Travis talking to Wendell beside her car. An angry expression hardened Coral's sharp features. It was plain the two were arguing.

Wendy's eyes grew round as she relished more gossip. "I wonder what Wendell Bixby thinks about Patrick's return? A city councilman running for mayor can't be thrilled to have his fiancée's unhappy past raked up again."

Knowing the town as well as she did, Shelby knew that was exactly what would happen. Wendy wasn't the only one who liked to gossip.

As Shelby stopped at her own car, she noticed a white slip of paper waving from beneath the driver's side wiper blade. Expecting it to be simply another Mother's Day Festival flyer, she unfolded it and stared at the message in astonishment.

The block-printed note said,

Keep your fat mouth shut about that night or you'll regret it.

THREE

A few minutes before nine o'clock the next morning, Shelby was still pondering the mystery of the note as she and Wendy walked toward the library door with Sarah Farley holding both their hands.

After going over it a million times, the note still didn't make sense. Why send her such a childish threat? Who could have written it? Keep her mouth shut about what night?

The night Leah went missing? The night Earl was murdered?

She'd gone over every minute of those nights with the police and the FBI a dozen times.

Mr. Peters had been babbling about not seeing something *that night*. Had his confused, paranoid mind focused on Shelby as a threat for some reason?

Or did the note refer to another night? The night of the Christmas party four years ago? The night of the bonfire ten years ago?

Charla Renault had certainly made it plain she wouldn't tolerate gossip about her son, but Shelby couldn't see Charla writing such a vague warning. She had no trouble delivering her threats in person.

That left Coral. Had she written the note? Shelby wouldn't put it past her, but why? It didn't make sense that after ten years Coral would suddenly start worrying that Shelby might talk about their confrontation the night of her alleged rape.

Was it because Patrick Rivers had returned?

Shelby inserted her key in the lock of the library door. The only explanation that made sense was that the note had been placed on her car by mistake.

She held the door open to let Wendy and Sarah precede her into the building as she struggled with the key. It always stuck. She would have to get a new one made one of these days.

"Can I go play?" Sarah looked at her for permission.

Shelby nodded and Sarah darted into the building. She already knew exactly where she wanted to go. The playroom where Shelby and Wendy held their Story Hour each Tuesday and Thursday morning at nine-thirty. A cast of character puppets lined the deep window seat in the room, waiting to be brought to life.

Once story time was over, Sarah's next favorite activity was helping Shelby empty the return book bin. Standing on a chair beside the metal container, Sarah would proudly hand over the books one by one until it was empty.

For Shelby, it was fun and yet sad to see Sarah acting so grown-up. Leah would be proud of her.

After those activities, Sarah would play on her special floor mat behind the counter until Clint arrived.

Shelby smiled as Sarah raced away, followed closely by Wendy. Keeping the child with her at the library for two mornings a week was Shelby's way of allowing Clint Herald a little breathing space.

The poor man had had parenthood thrust on him the same night his sister vanished. Shelby knew he was struggling to balance his construction business with Sarah's full-time needs and the ongoing search for Leah. Helping him by entertaining Sarah for a few hours was the least she could do.

The sound of approaching footsteps made Shelby look over her shoulder. Patrick Rivers was climbing the steps behind her.

The sudden skip of her heart caught her completely off guard. Feeling as flustered as she had when she was a college freshman, she struggled to get the key out of the lock.

"Let me." Closing his hand over hers, he turned it until it released.

"Thank you." She yanked the key free and pulled away from him. Her hand tingled from his touch. Warmth raced up her arm.

"My pleasure." He held the door open, allowing her to escape his overwhelming presence.

She crossed the entryway to the curved glass-fronted counter where her top picks for the week were displayed nestled in deep blue satin. Opening a small half door, she let herself behind the semicircular counter and closed the mahogany panel with a loud click. With the wide countertop between them she felt much more in control.

Patrick strolled in with an unhurried stride. Today he was wearing jeans and a sleeveless red denim shirt that exposed his tanned and muscular arms. Once again Shelby was reminded of a big cat on the prowl—all muscle and power waiting to explode. Her pulse kicked up another notch.

Please don't let me sound as breathless as I feel.

Pasting a smile on her face, she said, "Good morning. How may I help you?"

The noise of the outer door opening caused them both to glance in that direction. Two women with toddlers in tow entered the building. The quick glance the women exchanged when they noticed Patrick told Shelby they knew exactly who he was. They both herded their children back outside.

Shelby saw the slight slump to his shoulders before he turned back to her and laid a stack of books on the counter.

It must be awful to have people look at him with such suspicion and fear. She didn't want to feel sorry for him but she couldn't help it.

Did he regret the past? *Had he done it?*

He pushed the books toward her. "I found these at the house. I wanted to return them and pay whatever fine is due."

Opening the books, she found they were three months overdue. Did criminals return past-due library material? Why was it so hard to believe he'd done the things he was accused of?

"How much do I owe?" His grim face could have been carved out of stone.

The Patrick she remembered had smiled more. She suddenly missed that about him.

"Thank you for returning these. That will be one hundred dollars."

"What?" His eyes widened and locked with hers, a scowl cutting two deep creases between his dark brows.

Had she really said that? She didn't make jokes. She didn't flirt with her patrons. No, she certainly wasn't flirting.

She felt a rush of heat in her cheeks. "Just kidding. Our maximum fine is five dollars."

Scanning each book back into the system allowed her to avoid looking at him. When she did glance up, it was to see a smile twitching at the corner of his mouth.

Relaxing, she said, "You didn't check them out. I'm just happy you returned them. Of course, if you feel compelled to make a donation, I'll gladly accept. It's tax deductible."

He pulled his wallet from his hip pocket and thumbed through it. Selecting a bill, he laid a twenty on the counter. "Keep the change."

She smiled shyly. "Thank you. Let me get you a receipt."

* * *

Patrick leaned his elbows on the counter and watched Shelby as she pulled the necessary form from a drawer. His intention that morning had been to drop the books into the drive-up bin. It wasn't until he saw her walking across the parking lot that the desire to speak to her again had made him change his mind and come inside.

He was glad he had. Studying her, he tried to figure out why she was so appealing.

Her white blouse was simple and modest. She wore it tucked into the waistband of a narrow gray skirt. If she was trying to look the part of a librarian, she was succeeding.

She had a neat figure, but he'd seen far more stunning women who didn't spark his interest the way Shelby Mason did.

Maybe it was her red-gold hair. He liked the way she wore it long and loose. Was that it?

When she glanced up at him again, he suddenly knew the answer. The appeal was in her eyes.

A pale green-brown, they changed with the light and her mood. Sometimes they were green, sometimes almost gold. There wasn't any subterfuge or malice in her clear gaze. All he saw was kindness and curiosity and something he didn't have. A sense of inner peace.

People might overlook a small woman like Shelby Mason, but she wouldn't overlook anyone.

He glanced away, feeling an awkwardness that was unusual for him. Instead of staring at her, he looked around the room. The brightly painted walls and shoulder-high shelves didn't look anything like the library he remembered from his many trips here with his mother when he was a kid.

The place was brighter, more open. The colorful red carpet underfoot helped muffle the noise. If it had been here when he was young, he might have gotten in less trouble with Old Man Hillshire for being noisy.

Patrick studied Shelby once more. Maybe it was her presence that made the place shimmer with light.

Don't get fanciful. She wouldn't give you the time of day if she didn't have to.

"Will there be anything else?" she asked, handing him the receipt.

There wasn't, but he couldn't bring himself to leave. "There's been some changes in here. Looks nice."

"Thank you. I'm rather proud of my accomplishments."

She gestured toward a row of computers facing the wall. "We now have Internet access, books on tape, a regular series of speakers on Saturday afternoons and several special programs just for children."

"I noticed the little girl who came in with you. Is she yours?"

He suddenly disliked the idea that she belonged to someone else. He didn't want her to be happily married with children. He checked her left hand. She wasn't wearing a wedding band.

Shelby's smile faded. "No. Her name is Sarah Farley."

"Farley? Why does that name ring a bell?" Picking up a loose ink pen, he began to twirl it on the counter.

"Her father, Earl Farley, was murdered and her mother has been missing for the last three months."

He'd seen a few headlines about that in the newspapers at the house. "That must be rough on the kid."

He glanced toward the area where Sarah was making an elephant puppet romp over the other toys. Wendy was setting out small, red plastic chairs in a semicircle around a stage.

He knew what it was like to lose a mother. At least he'd had more years with his. A kid as young as Sarah wouldn't have memories to cling to.

"It's hard to say how much she really understands," Shelby

continued quietly. "She still asks for her mother, especially when she gets upset. It breaks my heart when that happens."

"Her mother was a friend of yours?"

"Is," Shelby stated firmly as she raised her chin. "Her mother *is* a friend of mine."

"After three months, you don't think she's going to come waltzing back into town, do you?"

"If she can—she will."

The conviction in Shelby's words touched him. What would it be like to have someone believe so strongly in him?

"I'm just saying it isn't likely."

"I know. I pray the FBI will find her. I pray she'll come home safe and sound. I pray she'll walk in here and smother Sarah with hugs and kisses. I get up every day with faith in my heart that today will be that day God brings her back to us."

Patrick knew her faith in God's help was misplaced but couldn't bring himself to say it to her face. "Why is the FBI looking into the case?"

"The mayor requested their help. Loomis has changed more than you might guess. We've had three murders here since the first of the year."

"Three?" He was surprised.

"Angelina Loring and Dylan Renault were both murdered shortly after Earl Farley."

Patrick gave a low whistle. "Dylan Renault, of the Renaults? I'll bet that shook up the town. Wealthy playboy meets fitting end?"

She scowled at him. "Being shot in the back is not a fitting end for anyone."

He tipped his head, acknowledging he was wrong. "Point taken."

Funny that he didn't want her thinking he was crass. Generally, he didn't care what anyone thought. Why was it important that she think well of him? He'd be gone from this town in a week or so and he'd never see her again.

He straightened, determined to ignore the nagging little voice that told him to stick around and get to know her better. Women were trouble. Even pretty librarians. He'd learned that lesson all too well.

"I should go before the PTA starts boycotting the building."

"They won't," she said quickly. "Don't you remember what's coming up?"

Did she want him to stay? Against his better judgment, he allowed himself to be persuaded. "What?"

Shelby bit the inside of her lip. What was she doing trying to prolong this conversation? Was she reliving some teenage fantasy? It was almost ridiculous how much she felt compelled to keep him here.

"The Mother's Day Festival is right around the corner. No one is going to make waves until after the Mother of the Year winner is announced."

She had work to do. She shouldn't be standing here chatting with him. Other patrons were coming in with their children. Story time was the highlight of her week. She loved showing kids the wonders of a book and watching their imaginations take flight.

Only, here she stood, making sheep eyes at Patrick Rivers instead of getting ready for her role as Mother Goose. Talk about pathetic. Why couldn't she let go of this silly infatuation with the man?

Maybe she should see Jocelyn as a patient instead of for coffee.

"So Loomis still has that stupid pageant?" There was no disguising the smirk in his voice.

She bristled in defense of the town. "It's a tremendous honor to win Mother of the Year. There's been a lot of talk about canceling it because of all that's happened, but I hope they don't."

"I remember the pageant as a battle for bragging rights between the Renaults and the Pershings. Has that changed?"

Ducking her head, she acknowledged he was right. "Not as much as some might like, but this year Ava Renault and Max Pershing are both working on the committee. They'll see that it's kept fair and square."

Shelby looked up and was surprised at the change that came over Patrick's face. His features hardened into a mask of barely controlled anger.

For the first time she found herself frightened of him. Here was a dangerous man. She took a step back. What had she said to make him so angry?

He noticed her withdrawal and relaxed slightly. With a nod to her he said, "I should get going."

"Of course."

Shelby turned away with relief to open the book drop bin beneath the window. As she raised the lid, a long black shape slithered onto the floor and coiled in front of her.

A scream tore from her throat.

FOUR

Patrick couldn't believe his eyes when he saw the snake land at Shelby's feet. Raising its head, it reared back and opened its jaws, revealing a puffy white mouth and needle-sharp fangs.

Her scream sent adrenaline spiking into his blood.

He vaulted over the counter and swept Shelby into his arms. The deadly cottonmouth struck his heel, twisting its head to drive its fangs and venom deep.

Depositing Shelby's slight frame on the countertop, he reached down and grabbed the snake behind the head before it could detach itself from the thick leather of his boot and try a higher strike.

At least three feet long and capable of inflicting serious harm, the moccasin hissed loudly and thrashed in Patrick's grasp.

His first instinct was to fling it away, but he couldn't allow it to escape into the main part of the library. After checking his limited options, he lifted the lid of the book bin and dropped the snake back inside, slamming the lid closed.

"It bit you!" Shelby, white and shaking, slipped from her perch, but her knees buckled and he was forced to catch her yet again.

"I'm fine. All it got was a mouthful of my boot."

Holding her close, he felt his danger-heightened senses take rapid inventory of the frightened woman in his arms. She trembled in his grasp as she clung to him.

The top of her head barely reached his chin. Her ginger hair, fine and sleek where it spilled over his arms, smelled of vanilla. Her rapid breathing warmed the skin of his throat and sent his already-pounding pulse shooting higher.

She tilted her face up to his. The pupils of her eyes were dilated with fear. Her delicate lips parted ever so slightly. "Thank you," she whispered.

He wanted to go on gazing into her eyes, holding her close, breathing in her scent. The urge to kiss her stunned him with its intensity.

Careful, he cautioned himself, reining in his emotions. She wasn't for him. The last thing he needed was to get involved with another woman from this town—even if his instincts were pushing him to ignore his own good sense.

The sound of running feet made him look up. Her friend came flying down the center aisle yelling, "Get your hands off her, you beast. I'm calling the police."

Do one good turn and what did it get him? He dropped his hands to his sides, fists clenched in resentment.

Shelby turned away from him. "No, Wendy, it's not what you think."

Wendy, gripping the other side of the counter, narrowed her eyes. "If he hurt you—"

"He saved me." Shelby pushed her hair back with one shaky hand. "Someone put a snake in the return book bin— a cottonmouth."

"What?" Wendy's wide-eyed gaze shot to the lid of the container.

"When it slithered out, it tried to strike me. Mr. Rivers jumped in the way and it bit his boot instead."

Shelby turned her gaze back to his. "I think I owe you my life."

"I saved you a trip to the emergency room, nothing more."

"What a sick joke. Why would someone do that?" Wendy demanded.

Patrick expected Shelby to agree, but instead an odd look darted across her face.

His curiosity reared its head much the same way the snake had. "Why would someone do that, Miss Shelby?"

Her eyes slid away from his. "I don't know."

She wasn't being entirely truthful. He could see it in her eyes. What did someone like Shelby Mason have to hide?

Shelby wished Patrick would leave. His dark eyes studied her every move as they waited for the sheriff and animal control to arrive. She had gone to sit with Sarah while Wendy put up a large Out of Order sign over the outside slot of the book return.

Normally, Sarah would have been the one to open the book bin.

Shelby closed her eyes in a brief prayer.

Thank you, Jesus, for letting me be the one to open it today. For putting Patrick here to save me.

Had this been an attempt to harm Sarah? Did it have to do with Earl's murder or Leah's disappearance?

Clint and Jocelyn were afraid Sarah may have seen something the night her father was murdered, and the FBI had already foiled one kidnapping attempt on her.

Did the unknown killer believe Sarah was a threat, or was this related to the note on Shelby's windshield?

Keep your fat mouth shut about that night or you'll regret it.

Had Shelby put Sarah in danger just by having her near? She shuddered at the thought.

A dozen young mothers with a contingent of noisy pre-schoolers were gathered in the play area. Shelby quietly explained to the women that a snake had found its way in but had been secured. It didn't surprise her that the majority of them took such an announcement in stride. Loomis, with its close proximity to the bayou, had its share of unwelcome reptile visitors every year.

The animal control officer was first on the scene. He quickly captured the snake and, to everyone's relief, secured it in a large bag with the intention of releasing it back into the wild where it belonged.

When the sheriff finally arrived, Shelby sent Wendy to begin the program and met with him in her small office behind the counter.

Sheriff Reed pulled out his notebook with a heavy sigh as Shelby began to relate the event. It wasn't until she mentioned Patrick's part that the officer showed the first spark of interest.

"Do I know you?" He furrowed his heavy brow and tipped his head to the side.

"We've met." Patrick's tone was dry, but she heard the animosity underneath.

"You're Dan Rivers's boy, aren't you? I didn't think you'd have the nerve to show your sorry carcass back in this town."

"It was Mr. Rivers's quick thinking that saved me today, Sheriff." If she hoped for a glimmer of gratitude for her defense of Patrick, she was doomed to disappointment.

Tapping his pen on the top of his notebook, Sheriff Reed asked, "And what were you doing here today, Rivers?"

"Returning books."

"You didn't drop them in the slot outside? Now, why was that?"

"I knew there was a fine to pay so I came inside."

"Don't think I'll rule you out because you've got a ready answer."

"You could dust the outside of the box for prints," Patrick suggested.

A small tic by his eye showed Sheriff Reed's annoyance. "Are you trying to tell me how to do my job?"

"Not at all. It was a simple suggestion."

"I reckon I'd get the prints of just about every bookworm in town. I think I'm done here, Miss Mason."

Patrick folded his arms over his chest. "You could ask me if I saw anyone loitering about when I drove up."

"I'm starting not to like you all over again, Rivers."

"The feeling is mutual, Sheriff."

Shelby interrupted their glaring match. "Patrick, did you see someone loitering outside?"

"A skinny little guy with red hair and thick glasses. I assumed he was homeless by the look of his clothes. He took off when I rode up."

Did he mean Chuck Peters? She had seen Chuck on the street when she found the note. Could he have done this? He'd certainly been disturbed in the park the previous morning.

It was easier to imagine Chuck putting a snake in the book slot than anyone else she knew. The only other person she could think of who might want her to keep quiet was Coral Travis. Coral picking up a snake was a sight Shelby was pretty sure she'd never see.

The sheriff addressed Shelby. "I know it's a day early, but this has all the earmarks of an April Fool's Day prank, Miss Shelby. I'll look into it, but I don't think I'll find much."

Shelby hesitated to say more in front of Patrick's intense scrutiny, but when the sheriff started to leave, she blurted out, "There's something else."

Sheriff Reed paused and looked over his shoulder. "And what would that be?"

"Yesterday I received a threatening note. It was left on the windshield of my car."

He turned back and eyed her curiously. "Exactly what did this note say?"

"It warned me to keep my mouth shut about that night, or I'd regret it."

"What night would that be?"

"It didn't say and I have no idea. I thought I should mention it in light of what happened here today."

Surely knowing about the note would make the sheriff suspect that someone other than Patrick was responsible for the snake.

"I'd like to see this note."

Suddenly, her actions yesterday seemed foolish. "I didn't keep it," she admitted. "It seemed like such a childish threat that I wadded it up and threw it away."

"I see."

She had the feeling the man didn't believe her. "I wouldn't make up such a thing. My cousin, Wendy, was with me."

"And she read the note?"

"No. I didn't show it to her. I told you, it seemed silly at the time."

"All right. If you get anything like that again, don't throw it away. Call my office."

"With the murder of my son still unsolved, Sheriff Reed, I'm surprised to find you wasting your time on such trivial matters." Charla Renault glared at the officer as she drove her wheelchair toward the counter.

Shelby knew a moment of pity for the man as he muttered an apology.

Mrs. Renault cut him off with a wave of her hand. "I'm

here to speak with Miss Mason. If you've concluded your business, of course."

"I reckon I'm done here. Miss Shelby, Mrs. Renault." The sheriff nodded at them, then turned to Patrick.

"I expect you to be leaving town soon. We don't cotton to the likes of you here."

"I don't much *cotton* to this town, Sheriff, but I'll leave when I'm ready and not before."

Shelby almost gasped at his audacity.

Reed's eyes narrowed, but he ignored the taunt and left.

Charla looked Patrick up and down and then dismissed him. She graced Shelby with a cool smile. "You look a trifle pale, Miss Mason."

"I had a small fright. It's nothing, I assure you. How may I be of assistance?"

"I thought perhaps we could discuss the plans y'all have for my son's memorial." With a twist of the lever by her right hand, she turned her wheelchair and began rolling away, leaving Shelby with no choice but to follow.

"I haven't yet formulated a complete plan, Mrs. Renault." To her surprise, Patrick fell into step behind them.

She was grateful for his help, but his presence made her jumpy. She could still feel his strong arms lifting her to safety.

"I didn't expect you would have," Charla replied without looking back. "I merely wanted to point out things I'd find unacceptable."

She stopped at the shelf where some of the current best-selling novels were on display. "For instance, I wouldn't want to see my money going to purchase more trash like this."

Patrick stepped in front of her and picked up a thriller. He opened the cover. "I've read this one. It's good. You should try it."

Shelby wanted to grab him by the collar and yank him out

of the way. Saving her life was one thing. Deliberately mocking the woman who proposed to give the library a large sum of money was something else altogether.

"I'm not surprised someone like you would think so." Charla drove forward toward the children's area.

Shelby grabbed Patrick's arm and snapped, "What are you doing?"

"She's making you jump like a lapdog for a biscuit."

"I'm not anyone's lapdog just because I speak to my elders in a civil tone."

"You mean, your 'betters'? She's not, you know. Just because she comes from an old family with money doesn't make her more important than you."

Shelby's eyebrows shot up. She opened her mouth to deny his charge but realized she did subconsciously think of the Renault family as superior to her own.

"I think you should leave now, Mr. Rivers. I'm grateful for your quick thinking and bravery this morning, but I have work to do."

Patrick replaced the thriller and picked up a new romance novel. "Don't let me keep you. I'll just browse awhile until I find something I'd like to check out."

"I'm sorry, but you have to be a resident to get a library card. You won't be able to check anything out."

He smiled at her. "In that case, I'll just read it here."

After walking to a small seating area, he settled himself in an easy chair and opened the novel.

Deciding that ignoring him was her best move, Shelby hurried after Mrs. Renault.

Charla had stopped just outside the area where Wendy was finishing up her puppet show. As Wendy bowed, the children and their mothers broke into applause.

One of the younger toddlers who came twice a week broke

into a wide smile and waved chubby fingers at Shelby. "Shelzie, read more!"

Sarah frowned at the little boy and shook her head. "That's Shelby, not Shelzie."

Rising from her place on the rug, Sarah raced to Shelby. Throwing one arm around her legs, Sarah held up her toy for inspection. "See my monkey?"

A second later, Sarah noticed that Mrs. Renault had wheeled closer. The three-year-old's almond-shaped green eyes grew wide. She leaned into Shelby. In a small voice, Sarah said, "Bad lady."

Already embarrassed, Shelby heard Patrick's smothered laugh turn into a cough. She was sure Mrs. Renault heard it, too.

Shelby placed a comforting hand on Sarah's head. "Honey, she's not a bad lady. I'm sorry, Mrs. Renault. Sarah has been much more shy with strangers since…recent events."

Sarah had also become terrified of anyone with red hair except Shelby since her father's death. The child's aversion to redheads was just one more piece in the jigsaw puzzle of events surrounding her father's murder and her mother's disappearance.

Charla studied Sarah intently. Shelby knew speculation about Dylan and Leah had been fueling the local rumor mill since Dylan's funeral. Was Charla wondering if this child was her granddaughter? Was she searching for a resemblance?

Swinging her wheelchair around abruptly, Charla said, "I certainly don't want my money used to entertain the children of bored housewives and trailer trash. I think I've made a mistake in including the library in my list of donation possibilities."

Shelby beckoned for Wendy to come and take Sarah, then hurried after Mrs. Renault to salvage the moment.

"I'm sure that I can find or develop a program that will meet with your approval, Mrs. Renault. The library has a great deal to offer the community. We have a media center for Internet access. We have a program that delivers reading material to shut-ins and a circulating exchange program with the local schools. I can promise we'll put the funds to good use."

Stopping, Charla looked over her shoulder. "Very well, Miss Mason. I'll keep an open mind until the board meeting."

She scowled at Patrick and then at the rowdy children being hustled outside by their mothers. "My family has occupied a prominent place in the history of Louisiana for generations. Please keep that in mind when developing your project proposal."

"Yes, Mrs. Renault."

Shelby released a deep sigh of relief when Mrs. Renault was finally out the door.

"I don't know which one is scarier," Patrick said at Shelby's elbow, "the snake or the old dragon."

Since her train of thought had been running along that very same track, Shelby didn't chide him for his comment.

Wendy came to stand beside Shelby. "Clint just came in."

Shelby nodded. "I'd better talk to him."

Turning away, she walked to the front of the building where Sarah's uncle stood waiting with Sarah in his arms. The worried look never seemed to leave his dark eyes these days.

Shelby didn't want to add to his burden, but Sarah's safety came first. Forcing a smile, she said, "Hello, Clint."

He nodded at her. "Wendy told me what happened. Do you think it was a prank?"

"I hope so, but I can't be sure. Either way, it could have been deadly serious."

His arms tightened around his niece. "Is this ever going to end?"

Reaching up, Shelby brushed back Sarah's hair. "I adore having her with me, but if anything had happened to her today, I don't know how I would've forgiven myself."

"I know she loves coming here, but I think it would be best if she stayed with me for the foreseeable future. This is such a public place. People come and go all the time. You can't watch everyone. Until this killer is brought to justice, I'd feel better keeping Sarah close."

"Of course. I understand." She walked with him to the door.

"Thanks for your help, Shelby. It means a lot to me."

She laid a hand on Clint's shoulder. "I'm keeping you in my prayers."

He nodded and left the building. With a heavy heart, Shelby watched him walk out. He was suffering so much.

Please, Lord, send him Your comfort.

Turning around, she found Patrick watching her intently.

Meeting his gaze, she asked, "What else can I do for you, Mr. Rivers?"

His dark brooding presence sent waves of awareness racing up her skin. The air became charged with electricity when he stepped close. She was glad when Wendy walked up beside her.

He said, "I've been going through some things at the house, and I came across a collection of books my mother owned. Some of them are pretty old, but I'm not sure if they are worth anything. I was wondering if you could suggest someone to evaluate them."

"If you bring them in here, I can certainly tell you if they are valuable."

"I would, but there are hundreds of them."

"Hundreds?" Shelby wasn't sure she heard him correctly.

"Several hundred at least."

"I see."

"Maybe you could drop by the house and take a look at them during your free time?" he suggested. His mocking gaze told her he knew she'd refuse.

"All right, I will." She wasn't afraid of him—exactly.

Surprise flashed in his eyes, but he recovered quickly. Crossing his arms, he leaned back slightly. "When?"

There was no turning back from the challenge in that one word. Lifting her chin, she said, "Tomorrow, after the library closes."

He glanced from Wendy's shocked face back to Shelby. "I'll understand if you change your mind."

"I won't. You saved my life today. It's the least I can do in return." That was as good an explanation as any for her insanity.

"See you then." His mocking half smile sent butterflies tumbling through her stomach.

As he walked out the door, Wendy grabbed Shelby's arm and spun her around. "Are you crazy? You absolutely cannot go to that man's house."

"I'm not insane. I'm not going alone." Shelby smiled brightly at her cousin. "You're coming with me."

FIVE

When Patrick answered the knock on his door late the next afternoon he had trouble disguising his surprise—and his pleasure.

He hadn't expected Shelby to actually show up.

He figured she would think better of her offer or that her friends would talk her out of coming. Yet here she was, standing on his porch, looking adorable and nervous. Not quite as nervous as Wendy, who was clutching Shelby's arm as if she might have to wrestle Shelby away from him at any second.

Movement next door caught Patrick's eye. He saw Wyatt unloading a cooler from the back of his pickup. Two young boys, one about six and the other a head shorter than his big brother, were pulling fishing poles out of the bed.

Wyatt's concentration wasn't on his work. His eyes were fastened on Patrick's house.

Once again, bitterness cut deep. How long would it take to convince his friend or this town that a woman was safe with him?

The answer was never. He wouldn't waste his breath trying to change that perception. When he left town this time, he'd never be back.

He nodded to the two women but found his gaze drawn to

Shelby's face, to her eyes and the kindness he sensed more than saw in them. "Thanks for coming. I appreciate this."

She smiled softly. "No problem. I love books, in case you couldn't tell that by my job."

"But we can't stay long," Wendy added quickly. "My husband is waiting for us. He knows I came here with my cousin."

A wry smile pulled at the corner of his mouth. "I've been reading through some of the old newspapers. Loomis isn't as safe as it looks. Even before I arrived."

"Where are the books?" Shelby asked.

Patrick turned and walked down the hallway, leaving the women to come in or not. At the door to his mother's sewing room, he opened it and stepped back. "I went through a few of the boxes, but I honestly have no idea if what I'm looking at is just old or old and valuable."

Shelby's eyes widened at the stacks of packing crates and cardboard containers filling the room. "These are all full of books?"

"I'm not sure," he admitted. "The first few had some clothes, but the rest have been books."

"Wow. I thought you were kidding about there being a hundred." She stepped into the room and Wendy slipped in with her, glaring at Patrick.

Shelby sank to the floor and opened the lid of the first box. "Oh, my."

"What?" Wendy demanded, peering closer.

Lifting out a slim, dark-red leather volume, Shelby passed it to Wendy, who immediately sank to the floor. "*The Memoirs of Sadie Winslow.* I don't believe it!"

"Who is Sadie Winslow?" With his hands stuffed in the front pockets of his jeans, Patrick leaned nonchalantly against the doorjamb.

"First edition?" Shelby asked.

Wendy carefully opened the binding. "Yes, 1876. Oh, my. It's signed," she added with a squeal.

A huge smile wreathed Shelby's face as she glanced up at Patrick. "Sadie Winslow was a freed slave in New Orleans. Her memoirs helped pinpoint injustices in the property laws at the time."

"So it's valuable?"

"This copy has a few condition flaws, but it's still worth several hundred dollars. If this is any indication of what your mother collected, she had fine taste."

"She loved books and history."

Shelby pulled the next novel from the box and ran her hand gently over the cover. "I know the feeling. There's just something about opening one. I guess it's the mystery. What will the author reveal? Where in the world will the words take me? What secrets, what puzzles will be answered?"

The reverence in her tone reminded him so strongly of his mother that a lump pushed its way up in his throat.

"What are these?" Wendy had opened another box. She held up a package covered with Christmas wrapping paper.

She passed it to Shelby, who read the note attached and then held it up to Patrick. "It's for you."

Sudden tears pricked the back of his eyes and he blinked them back. His mother had passed away a few weeks before Christmas his junior year in high school.

He vividly remembered that first holiday without her. There hadn't been a tree or gifts. His stepfather had retreated into his room that day and hadn't come out until the next morning.

Patrick took the package from Shelby's hand and walked down the hall to the kitchen, where he stood staring at the last gift his mother had given him. Feeling the pain of her loss all over again.

Carefully, he undid the brittle wrapping paper and laid it aside. It was copy of *The Adventures of Tom Sawyer*, an early edition, with beautiful color plates. She had tucked a note inside.

Merry Christmas, Darling. May your life be filled with many adventures. Love forever, Mom.

His life had been filled with adventures all right, but not the kind he would have wanted his mother to know about.

"I found this one for someone named Wyatt." Shelby stood in the doorway holding out another gift-wrapped book. Dust smudged her cheek.

Repressing the urge to reach out and brush the dirt from her face, he focused on the gift instead. "That would be Wyatt Tibbs."

"You two were friends in college, weren't you?"

"Since before grade school."

"I'm sure he'd like to have this."

Patrick took the book from her hand. "Our friendship didn't exactly thrive after…you know."

She rubbed her palms on her pant legs. "I'm sorry."

He shrugged. "It is what it is."

"Where did you go—after you left here?"

"Around."

"That doesn't tell me much. Perhaps I should have asked where you ended up?"

"Los Angeles."

"L.A., that sounds exciting."

He tipped his head to one side. "Does it?"

"To someone who never made it out of Loomis, yes. What do you do there?"

"I fix motorcycles."

It was her turn to look skeptical. "Really?"

"Being a grease monkey isn't a good enough profession?" He kept his voice level with difficulty.

"Of course it is. Any job is worthwhile if you love it."

He could have let it drop there but found himself wanting to share more about himself. Should he risk it?

"I started out fixing bikes for a guy named Carl Wolf. He runs a custom bike shop in L.A. He always claimed he saw potential in me. Before long he had me in night school learning about design and fabrication."

"That makes sense. I remember seeing some of the sketches you used to draw."

He chuckled. "I'm afraid none of them would have stood up to a road test. It's odd you should mention those. You must have a great memory."

Shrugging, she asked, "Did you design the bike outside?"

"Yes."

"It's really cool. Very powerful looking. Very feline."

"You have a good eye."

She looked down, embarrassed by his praise.

"Why didn't you leave Loomis?" he asked, wondering how someone as sweet as Shelby had remained that way in the oppressive town.

She shrugged. "I have roots that hold me here."

"Roots hold down trees, not people. People are free to move on."

"Not everyone wants to move on."

"No, not everyone—but for some, it's the only choice." He didn't normally talk about himself. What was it about this woman that made him open up?

A shriek rent the air, followed quickly by Wendy's excited voice. "Shelby! Y'all got to see this!"

Turning, Shelby hurried back to her cousin. Although he should have been relieved that their private conversation was at an end, he wasn't.

Troubled by the conflicting emotions Shelby evoked in him, he followed more slowly. He stopped at the door to the room where Wendy sat looking into a large box. Her eyes were as round as saucers.

"What is it?" Shelby demanded, dropping down beside her.

"Refléxions sur la Campagne du Général André Jackson by Bernard Marigny…first edition…wonderful condition. Oh, what a find. Where on earth did your mother get this?"

"It's hard to say. She loved looking for books at estate sales. She went prowling through old bookstores in New Orleans every chance she got. Who is Bernard Marigny?"

"Only the founder of our fair city and a famous Renault ancestor," Wendy supplied.

Shelby slowly lifted the book out of the box. "I think this is exactly the kind of thing Mrs. Renault would like."

"What do you mean?" Patrick asked.

"Mrs. Renault is considering making a large donation to the library in her son's name," Shelby explained, "if we can show her we can develop a suitable memorial."

"Like a special collection of research books on Louisiana history?" Wendy's eyes sparkled. "I think she just might go for that."

"The Dylan Renault Research Center for Loomis History and Genealogy." Excitement shimmered in Shelby's voice. "We could use that big storeroom on the east end of the second story. It would be perfect—a dedicated space with limited access."

"It's close to the elevators, and it wouldn't take much to make it wheelchair accessible," Wendy added.

"How much is the book worth?" Patrick asked.

Shelby and Wendy both looked up at him. "Historically, it's an important work," Shelby said.

"So, how much? A couple hundred bucks?"

"At least."

"Great. Who would buy it?"

"There are rare-book dealers in New Orleans, but if Mrs. Renault gives our library the money, we would be able to offer you fair market value for it."

"How soon?"

"I'm not sure. A few weeks or a month."

He shook his head. "Thanks, but no thanks. I'm not hanging around that long."

Shelby raised one eyebrow. "I guess donating the copy to us would be out of the question?"

For a second, he was tempted to do just that. He wanted to see those gold-green eyes of hers alight with happiness, but he quickly discarded the notion. He needed every dollar he could raise. "I don't think so. Is there anything else of value in these boxes?"

Rising, Shelby dusted off her hands. "It will take several more hours to go through all of these, but I'm afraid we don't have time to do it today."

Wendy jumped to her feet as if afraid of being left alone with him. "Yes, we should get going."

"I can come by again tomorrow evening," Shelby stated firmly, meeting his gaze without flinching. "If that's all right with you?"

Was she trying to prove she wasn't afraid of him, or was she genuinely interested in helping him?

"I'll be here." The rise in his spirits at the thought of seeing her again surprised him. He stepped aside to let the women leave.

Don't go getting attached to her. It'll only bring trouble.

Following them to the front door, he leaned one shoulder against the square porch column as he watched them descend the steps. He couldn't help but notice the sway of Shelby's long hair down her back.

Sunlight caught the different colors of red, revealing a multitude of highlights. As she turned to face him once more, the breeze blew a strand across her face. She reached up and tucked it behind her ear.

How would her hair look blowing out behind her as she rode his bike? He imagined the way the ends would whip and curl as if they had a life of their own. His fingers itched to reach out and touch it.

Just beyond her, he caught sight of Wyatt and his wife in the front yard. Camera in hand, Mrs. Tibbs was busy snapping photos of the boys each holding up a large catfish. Wyatt spoke in her ear and then said something to the boys. The kids carried their prizes around the side of the house.

Patrick straightened and shoved his hands deep in his front pockets. Shelby followed his gaze. She lifted her hand in a brief wave, and Wyatt's wife waved back.

Looking at Patrick, Shelby said, "You should give him the present your mother left for him."

"Why?" A book wouldn't heal what lay between them.

"Because God moves in mysterious ways," Shelby said softly.

Her comment pulled his attention back to her. "What's that supposed to mean?"

"That you were meant to find your mother's gifts today. It's up to you what you do with them. I'll be back after the library closes tomorrow."

He motioned with his chin toward Wendy, waiting beside their car. "Don't forget to bring your watchdog."

Shelby grinned and giggled. The sudden sweet sound made his breath catch in his throat.

She didn't seem to notice the effect she had on him. "I doubt I'll be able to get out the door without her and her trusty can of mace."

"From what I've read in the old newspapers here, she has the right idea."

The laughter left her eyes to be replaced by worry. "Perhaps she does."

He was sorry he had reminded her of her fright and of the loss of her friend. "Take care."

Smiling slightly, she nodded. "I will."

As she and Wendy drove away, Patrick watched Wyatt and his wife continuing their yard work.

It doesn't matter what Wyatt or anyone else thinks of me. I'm not staying in Loomis. I've got a life away from this hole.

But it did matter what Shelby thought of him. She would ask about the gift when she came back.

Turning abruptly, he reentered the house. The red-and-green striped package still sat on the kitchen counter. He walked over and picked it up. What book had his mother chosen for his best friend all those years ago? His stepfather had obviously packed it away. Why hadn't he given it to Wyatt?

"Because God wants me to do it, according to Miss Shelby." Patrick tried to muster the appropriate sarcasm but didn't quite manage it. She had spoken with such conviction.

Picking up the package, he hefted the weight of it in his hand. It would only take a second to open it, to rip away the colorful paper now brittle with age. Maybe it was another valuable book. Something he could sell and get one step closer to his dream.

His mother's face floated before his mind's eye. This was her gift to Wyatt. He had no right to it. Before he could change his mind, he walked out the door and down the steps. Wyatt was hosing the mud from his truck tires. When he caught sight of Patrick, he turned off the nozzle.

At the fence, Patrick waited as Wyatt walked slowly toward him. He held out the package.

Wyatt looked at it but didn't take it. "What's this?"

"I found it when I was going through some stuff. The card says it's for you."

"Me?"

"From my mom. It looks like she bought you something before she died."

Slowly, Wyatt reached out and took the package. A guarded look settled over his face. "Your mom was always good to me."

"Your folks were always good to me."

An awkward silence stretched on, but neither man moved. The boy came running out of the house but slowed when he saw his father with a stranger. The tyke was the spitting image of his father with dark hair and dark eyes.

Patrick smiled at him. "Did you catch that big catfish all by yourself?"

The boy's eyes widened. "Yeah, and I put my own worms on, too."

Patrick chuckled at his enthusiasm. "I'll bet you caught him from the end of the dock at your dad's cabin out in the bayou. Right?"

He bobbed his head. "Yeah! How'd you know?"

"I caught a few from that spot myself."

"Mark, go on back in the house." Wyatt tipped his head in that direction.

"Okay, Dad. Mom says you'd better come skin them catfish before they start stinkin'."

"I'll be right in."

As the boy ran back the way he'd come, Patrick struggled with a touch of envy. At least Wyatt's life had turned out well.

Patrick motioned to the book in his friend's hands. "I just thought you should have it."

Turning away, Patrick walked to back to the porch. When he glanced back, Wyatt was still standing with the unopened gift in his hands.

SIX

Early on Friday afternoon, Shelby sat eating her lunch on a stone bench situated beneath the spreading branches of a dogwood. The tree, one of eight that bordered the side of the library, was heavy with blooms and the air was sweet with their fragrance. Overhead, the sky shone crystalline-blue without a cloud in sight. For a change, the air was free of the pressing humidity.

As she munched her tuna salad sandwich, Shelby mentally tried to prepare her presentation to the library board and Mrs. Renault but instead found her thoughts occupied by Patrick.

When she and Wendy had arrived at his house after work the previous day, he'd been waiting for them. Seated in a chair with his boots propped up on the porch railing, he looked like a man without a care in the world, but it was plain that he'd been busy. The yard had been freshly mown and there were a half dozen bags of trash out by the curb.

He'd let them into the house and then took off on his bike—like it didn't matter that she was there.

Shelby had wanted to share her discoveries with him. Wanted to see his eyes light up and listen to stories about his life in L.A. Instead, she and Wendy had spent the three hours discovering at least another dozen books of value among his mother's collection. Patrick never returned while they were there.

It shouldn't bother her—but it did.

Stuffing the uneaten portion of her sandwich back in the brown paper bag at her side, she scolded herself for spending so much time and energy thinking about the man, about his motives, about his feelings.

Suddenly, as if conjured by her thoughts, he roared into the parking lot on his bike.

She started to lift her hand to wave but stopped herself. He didn't look in her direction. Instead, he marched with purposeful strides toward the town hall.

Disappointment settled over her.

Don't be a silly goose. Why would he be coming to see me? He didn't even bother to stick around when Wendy and I were at his house.

Shelby picked up her can of diet soda and took a long swig. As much as she prided herself on being logical, that didn't seem to be the case where Patrick Rivers was concerned.

A logical woman would avoid him like the plague. Shelby didn't understand the attraction that drew her to him. It might have started as a schoolgirl crush years ago, but this was something different. It was thrilling and frightening at the same time.

There was certainly plenty of gossip going around town about the man. To her shame, she listened, hoping to learn more about him. Most of what she heard was speculation about his alleged past crime.

The uncertainty of it gnawed at Shelby. Had he done it? Only one woman knew for certain.

Shelby didn't want him to be guilty.

Abruptly, Shelby set down the can she was holding. Coral

Travis worked in the town hall. Shelby stared at the second-story corner window of the building she knew was Coral's office.

Had Patrick gone to see her?

Shelby sent up a quick prayer for reconciliation. Both of them had suffered.

Propping her elbows on her knees, she waited and watched. She didn't have to wait long.

Patrick came storming out the town hall doorway with a fierce scowl on his face.

For a second, Shelby's courage wavered.

Okay, Lord, You put me on this bench today and You've all but dropped him in my lap. I'm not chasing after him. I'm trying to help my library and the people of this town.

She rose and started across the lawn

"Mr. Rivers," she called out loudly. "Do you have a moment?"

He stopped and stared at her. The scowl on his face didn't budge. "It seems I've got more time than I expected. What can I do for you?"

This didn't bode well for her request.

Shelby made her way between two parked cars and stopped on the opposite side of his bike. "I hope I'm not keeping you from something."

"You're not, but some people are." He glanced over his shoulder.

Shelby followed his gaze to see Coral Travis watching them from her window with a self-satisfied smile on her face. Reaching over, she tugged on a cord and the blinds dropped, cutting her off from their view.

Puzzled, Shelby said, "I don't understand."

Sighing, Patrick took a seat on his cycle. "I'm trying to get my stepfather's house on the market, but it seems there's a problem with the title."

Shelby frowned. "What kind of problem?"

"The property deed seems to have been misplaced. No clear title, no sale—until the records are found."

"I'm sorry to hear that, but I'm sure it won't take long to straighten out the problem."

"Right. And the moon is made of green cheese."

She didn't know what to say in the face of his deep sarcasm. Looking down, she bit her lip and crossed her arms.

"I'm sorry, Shelby, I shouldn't take my bad temper out on you."

"It must be frustrating for you having to stay in Loomis."

"I need to get back to L.A. I should have known something like this would happen. Nothing good has ever come out of this town."

"God's goodness is all around us. Even in Loomis."

"How can you say that, knowing your friend is still missing and three people are dead?"

"There is evil in the world, I'm not denying that. I'm only saying that more good than evil exists in our lives. Look for the good as hard as you look for the bad, Mr. Riv—Patrick. You'll find it."

He tilted his head to the side and studied her until she felt the color rising in her cheeks. "I'm glad you called me Patrick. Any more snakes in your book bin?"

"No. I think the sheriff was right. It was an April Fool's joke gone bad."

"Any more notes on your windshield?"

"No, and you don't have to point out every bad thing that's happened in my week to make your case."

"What case would that be?"

"That I refuse to see the bad things happening around me."

"Aren't you guilty of wearing rose-colored glasses?"

"No, I wear contacts, but they're not tinted."

He chuckled at that. "All right. I'll see good if I look for it. What did you need to talk to me about?"

"I was hoping you might reconsider donating some of your mother's books to our library. Especially the six journals and diaries from the eighteen hundreds that we found last night. They are one-of-a-kind works that provide a unique look into the lives of Louisiana people prior to the Civil War."

He shoved his hands in his jean pockets and leaned back. "You want them so you can impress Mrs. Renault with the start you've made to her son's legacy."

Shelby opened her mouth to protest but closed it quickly. "All right, I'm busted. Yes, I want to show that I have more than an idea. That I already have a collection started. It'll make more of an impression if she can look through some of the books and journals and see for herself how important it is to preserve our heritage."

"Mrs. Renault was busy making cutthroat business deals while my mother drove the length and breadth of this state saving 'our heritage' on a measly teacher's salary. Now you want me to hand it over *for nothing* so Charla Renault can hang her son's name on it?"

Feeling shamefaced, Shelby said, "You're right. I'm sorry."

Taking a deep breath, he countered her apology with one of his own. "No, don't be sorry. I'm having a bad day, and I'm taking it out on you. Mom might have liked the idea. Since I'm going to be in town for a little longer, I'll think about it."

Shelby brightened suddenly. "Hey, maybe Max Pershing could help you with your property deed. Max is a member of our church. His family owns the largest real estate firm in the area. I'm sure he deals with deeds and such all the time."

"I already have a Realtor from Covington."

"Yes, but Max is local and his family is—high powered. In this case, he might be able to help you more than an outsider."

"I thought the Renaults had all the political clout in this town."

"It's been about half-and-half, but Max just got engaged to Ava Renault, so he has that half covered, too."

Shaking his head, Patrick looked down. "Like *her* fiancé is going to help me."

"Why wouldn't he?"

He glanced up at her. "Are you that naive or don't you know?"

"Know what?"

"Ava Renault is the one who found me in bed with Coral. She's the one who first cried rape."

Patrick clenched his jaw so tightly his teeth ached. Reliving that night served no purpose. A promising football career, his reputation, his relationship with his friends and his stepdad, all of it had come to an end that night.

He studied Shelby's face. *Does she believe I'm guilty?*

Folding her arms over her chest, she looked truly distressed. "I didn't know Ava had anything to do with it."

If he explained, would she accept it as the truth?

He needed that. He needed someone to believe he was innocent.

If she didn't, after so much disappointment, he wasn't sure he could face it.

Take a chance. Tell her the truth.

If nothing else, it might help him to get the story off his chest. Maybe airing the whole thing would finally put to rest the bitterness that consumed him.

Glancing around the busy parking lot, he took her elbow and guided her toward the stone bench she had recently vacated. He might work up the nerve to tell Shelby, but he didn't want anyone else listening in.

Taking a seat on the bench, Shelby looked up at him. He didn't sit. Instead, he pushed his hands deep in his pockets again.

"Coral approached me at the after-game party that night. I was flattered out of my mind. She was way out of my league and I knew it."

He laughed bitterly. "Mix a victory party with too much alcohol and revved-up male hormones, and you get stupid instead of smart. No, who am I kidding? I never was that smart to begin with."

"I always thought you tried to hide your intelligence."

He cocked his head to one side. "Why would I do that?"

Raising her hands as if to balance them like scales, she said, "You know—jocks were cool—brainy was uncool."

He chuckled. Some of his tension drained away. "You were brainy."

Folding her hands in her lap, she nodded. "Which proves my point."

"You weren't uncool."

"Yes, I was, but you didn't notice because I was good at being invisible."

He'd spent the last ten years focused on how hard his life had been. He hadn't given much thought to how others had fared. Had he always been so selfish? "I'm sorry if I snubbed you."

Lifting her shoulders in a quick shrug, she said, "You didn't. If you'd rather not talk about that night, I understand."

"Like I said, I made some stupid decisions."

"Maybe it's time you forgave yourself for that."

"Are you my therapist now?"

"No, but I understand how we sometimes continue to blame ourselves long after we've forgiven someone else."

"If you think I've forgiven Coral or Ava Renault, you're wrong. Coral invited me to her dorm room of her own free will. We made love. I fell asleep. The next thing I know, the lights come on and Ava Renault is staring at me like I was that snake that tumbled out of your book bin.

"Coral sits up, takes one look at Ava and then starts babbling that she didn't know what happened or how I got in bed with her. She claimed the last thing she remembered was having a beer at the bonfire. That's when Ava blurted out that I must have slipped something in Coral's drink. I didn't even know what to say. I had no idea how to get those kind of drugs, but Coral latched on to the idea and ran with it. She started shouting that I must have given her something."

"Did you try to explain?"

"Of course I did, but by this time Ava had the phone in her hand. I can still hear her coolly saying she was reporting a rape. Thirty minutes later, I was on the way to the Loomis jail because what a Renault wants, a Renault gets in this town."

"Coral never recanted her statement?"

"No. There wasn't enough evidence to make a case. It was her word against mine. Let me tell you, once someone hangs that label on you, it never comes off. A week after I was released, the dean called me in to tell me my scholarship had been revoked. In case you missed it, the Renaults have a lot of pull in this town. The life I knew, the dreams I had, they vanished before my eyes."

"So you left Loomis."

"My stepfather threw me out. I couldn't get a job. What choice did I have?"

"Did you speak to Coral after that night?"

"Of course I tried, but I couldn't get past her self-appointed bulldog. Ava made sure I didn't 'bother' her roommate again."

"Ten years is a long time. Perhaps if you spoke to Coral now…"

He glanced over his shoulder at the town hall. "I think the missing deed makes it pretty clear that Coral has no interest in mending fences."

"You can't be sure she's behind that. It could be a simple clerical error. She may be willing to help clear your name."

"Can you see the wife of the next mayor standing up in front of everyone and admitting she lied? That she was a party to a false arrest?"

"If she has God in her heart, she can admit the truth."

"I don't believe God has anything to do with it."

"You aren't a believer?"

"God pretty much turned His back on me ten years ago, so I returned the favor."

"That isn't true. God never turns His back on anyone. We suffer, we are tested, we may never know why, but God is always with us."

"What makes you so sure?"

"Faith."

"You make it sound simple."

"Searching for faith is a lot like seeking the good in people. If you refuse to look, you won't find it."

He tipped his head to stare into her sympathetic eyes. "Do you believe my story?"

"Yes."

One simple word, yet it meant so much.

He filled his lungs with air, amazed to find the tight band of bitterness loosening its grip. After all this time, someone believed him.

"Thank you."

Such an inadequate phrase for the gratitude he wanted to express.

"You're welcome." Her eyes never left his.

He reached out and gently touched her cheek. "Has anyone told you how beautiful you are?"

At Patrick's words and gentle touch, Shelby's heart skipped a beat then raced madly. The look in his eyes sent warmth coursing through her body. The spicy scent of his aftershave mingled with the sweet perfume of the blossoms around her, creating a cocoon of splendor. He thought she was beautiful. Her adolescent daydreams all those years ago were nothing compared to the reality of this moment.

If only she could help him find his way back to God.

Smiling softly, she said, "I know I'm not that pretty. You're just being kind."

An inscrutable expression settled over his features. The warmth vanished from his eyes, replaced by cynicism. "You're far too trusting, Shelby."

Baffled by the change in his demeanor, she struggled to understand. "Why do you say that?"

"Your face is as easy to read as a first-grade book. I appreciate that you believe me, but don't go thinking that I'm kind or that you can reform me."

Embarrassed, Shelby rose to her feet, wanting only to escape. How stupid of her to read more into his touch than simple gratitude. "If you'll excuse me, I have to return to work."

Gathering the remains of her lunch, Shelby hurried toward the entrance of the library. Glancing back once, she saw he was still standing in the same spot, watching her.

SEVEN

"That man is outside again."

Shelby jumped at the sound of the hoarse whisper by her ear. Spinning around, she found the elderly Miss Maynard clutching the murder mysteries she'd checked out and casting nervous glances over her shoulder toward the door.

Following her gaze, Shelby's heart skipped a beat. Was it Patrick?

It wasn't.

Chuck Peters, dressed in dirty tan pants and a plaid shirt, stood at the base of the steps, panhandling as people walked by.

Disappointment sharp as a sliver from the old wooden shelves pierced her bubble of hope. What was she thinking? Patrick had no reason to come here. Especially after what he'd said last week.

During the past week she'd seen him only once. She'd gone with some friends to the local Italian restaurant. Patrick had been sitting alone at a table in the rear, studiously ignoring the veiled looks cast his way by other patrons.

Part of her wanted to march over and ask if she could join him, but she didn't have enough courage. Instead, she'd endured an uncomfortable meal knowing he was just across the room.

Had he managed to straighten out his problems with his property deed? If he had, he'd be leaving soon. The thought that she might never see him again lowered her already-low spirits.

"I don't like the looks of him." Miss Maynard made her disapproval clear.

"Do you carry books on Internet crimes?" a youthful male voice asked behind Shelby.

"Miss Mason, the sink in the bathroom is stopped up," someone called from the end of the aisle.

Shelby tore her gaze away from the door and cast a quick look at the people gathering around her.

Would this day ever end?

The library normally closed at five, but today was Thursday, the one day a week they stayed open until eight o'clock.

Tonight was the board meeting. Her one and only chance to convince Charla Renault the library deserved her donation.

Instead of concentrating on her presentation, all Shelby could do was think about Patrick.

"You should call the cops on him."

Shelby pasted a smile on her face as she turned to the tiny white-haired woman. Her cheeks actually ached with the effort. Even the children during Story Hour that morning had been restless and difficult to control.

"Mr. Peters is harmless, Miss Maynard."

Nodding to the young mother with a toddler on her hip and one more in tow, Shelby waved and called out, "Thank you, Mrs. Kelley, I'll see to the bathroom in a moment."

Next?

She smiled at the impatient young man shifting his weight from one foot to the other. All of fifteen years old, he was wearing a pair of hideous black baggy pants and a black T-shirt and sporting an earring in one ear.

"Internet crimes would be in aisle three unless you want fictional Internet crimes."

"Real crimes. I want to see how to outsmart the cops."

"I hope you aren't serious."

"Why?" he demanded with a scowl.

"Never mind. Is there something specific I can help you find?"

"No." The wannabe hoodlum sauntered away.

"Are you gonna call the cops or should I?" Miss Maynard demanded.

"The police won't be necessary, Miss Maynard. I'll speak to Mr. Peters. Would you like someone to walk you to your car?"

"Yes, thank you, Miss Mason. A body can't be too careful in this day and age. Horrible things have been happening right under our noses. Why the police can't solve these crimes is beyond me."

"Yes, I agree it's terrible." She lifted a hand to attract Wendy's attention. "Wendy, would you walk Miss Maynard to her car?"

Looking puzzled as she approached, Wendy nodded. "Sure."

Giving Wendy a sidelong glance, Miss Maynard scowled. "Y'all don't look like you'd be much help."

Wendy pulled a thin can from the pocket of her smock. "Don't worry, I'm armed with mace."

Miss Maynard's eyes lit up. "Where can I get some?"

"The police surplus store in Covington. It's just past the second stoplight on Lafayette Boulevard."

The two women walked outside. As they exited, Shelby was surprised to see Coral Travis enter.

Coral wasn't a library regular. Her reading tastes ran more toward glossy gossip magazines than novels. A stunning blonde with shoulder-length hair, she wore it styled to look artfully casual. Dressed today in a pale-blue linen suit jacket over a matching snug skirt with a slit halfway up one thigh, she managed to look cool and businesslike while maintaining an underlying impression of sensuality. The dark glasses she wore added to her air of mystery.

Why had she lied about her involvement with Patrick ten years ago? Perhaps now was the time to find out.

Giving the woman a brief nod of recognition, Shelby walked toward her. "What can I help you with, Coral?"

Pulling her sunglasses from her face, Coral looked around. "Is there someplace we can speak in private?"

"About what?"

"If I told you here, it wouldn't be private, would it?"

Leading the way to a small meeting room, Shelby waited until Coral walked in, then shut the door. "All right. What's this about?"

"I saw you outside with Patrick Rivers last week. The two of you looked very cozy."

"I saw you watching us. Does that make us even?"

"Don't be flippant."

Folding her arms, Shelby raised her chin. "Say what you came to say."

"Tell him to get out of town."

"Why should I?"

"The longer he stays here, the more the old gossip gets raked up and spread around. My fiancé Wendell is running for mayor next term. This kind of thing can hurt his career."

"Patrick might have been gone by now if someone hadn't *misplaced* the deed to his parents' property."

"He shouldn't profit from anything in Loomis."

Shaking her head sadly at Coral's animosity, Shelby did what she should have done back in college. "I don't know what your reason was for lying ten years ago, but enough damage has been done. Tell the truth."

Coral's eyes narrowed. "What do you mean?"

"Speak up and clear Patrick's name. You owe him that."

Coral's gaze crackled with fury. "He's guilty. He drugged me and took advantage of me."

"Coral, I was at the party, remember? I overheard you say you were going home with Patrick no matter what it took. I don't know what happened later, but I know you had your sights set on being with him that night."

He might have been a good football player but his family was white trash. "Why would I do that?"

"I'm not sure. I thought it was because you liked him. He was a football star, and you liked the limelight. If that wasn't the reason then tell me what was."

"I don't have to tell you anything. And if you breathe a word of that ridiculous story to anyone, you'll regret it."

Coral shouldered past Shelby and yanked open the door. Glancing back, she said, "This job is an appointment by the mayor. The next mayor can replace you. Remember that before you go spreading lies about me."

Shelby followed Coral to the doors as she marched out of the building. Chuck, begging money at the foot of the stairs, moved rapidly out of Coral's way. He looked up at Shelby with wide wild eyes. The poor little man looked even thinner than he had when she'd seen him the other day.

Walking down the steps, she asked gently, "Mr. Peters, have you been to see Reverend Harmon?"

Casting frantic glances in all directions, he shook his head and sidled closer. "You're in danger, Miss Shelby," he said in a loud whisper. He seemed truly frightened.

Fear crept up her spine, making her mouth dry and her heart race. "What are you talking about?"

He became ever more agitated, wringing his hands as he scanned the area. "I see things. I know things. You ain't safe."

"Are you saying someone wants to hurt me? Who?"

He took a step closer. "Did you tell where I was? Did you?"

"No. I didn't tell anyone." She moved toward the door, wishing she had availed herself of Wendy's mace.

"Don't go near the old Renault place," he shouted. "There's *evil* out in that swamp."

With that, he clamped his mouth shut and hurried away, his head bowed, his hands thrust deep in his pockets as if making himself a smaller target.

Shelby watched with relief as he disappeared into the park. Her pounding heart slowed. For the first time in her life, she had been truly frightened of the little man. Had she been wrong to assume he was harmless?

Why did he want her to stay away from the old Renault place? The crumbling ruin of a mansion at the edge of town was where Dylan Renault had been murdered. Angelina Loring's body had been discovered in the swamp nearby. Shelby certainly had no intention of prowling the property.

Were Chuck's frightening ramblings the result of his drinking, or did he really know something?

Patrick pulled to a stop on the quiet side street beside the library a few minutes before eight o'clock. The gray twilight was fading into darkness as low swirls of fog crept in from the swamp. The air hung heavy and thick with the damp smell of the bayou.

Turning off his bike, he sat and stared at the large brick building. Light poured from the wide arching windows behind the row of blooming dogwood trees.

The thought that he was making a fool of himself occurred to him yet again, but he wrestled it out of his way.

Opening one of his saddlebags, he removed a package he'd brought from the house. It was his way of apologizing to Shelby for his unkind remarks. She would never know how much he wanted to kiss her that day.

She would have slapped his face.

Or maybe not. He was more attracted to her than anyone he'd ever met. Which didn't make a bit of sense. A woman like her with a man like him? It would never work.

But she believed he was innocent.

He couldn't quite wrap his mind around that. Her faith in him was mind-boggling. He didn't know how to deal with it. One part of him said, "Get out of town before you hurt her." The other part of him wanted to stay and explore the sense of wonder he felt when he was near her.

His mouth twisted into a grimace. He was better at running than he was at staying.

Tucking the package under one arm, he started toward the building. As he did, he caught sight of someone near the rear of the structure.

The thick branches of the trees and the growing darkness obscured his view, but something about the furtive behavior of the individual made him stop to take a second look. When he did, the figure retreated around the corner and vanished.

Unease settled in the pit of his stomach. Something wasn't right. The memory of the snake at Shelby's feet propelled him forward to get a closer look.

Walking beneath the trees toward the back of the building, Patrick ducked under some of the low branches. The thick green grass underfoot was littered with white petals and muffled the sound of his footsteps. When he rounded the far corner of the library, he scanned the nearly empty parking lot. There was no one in sight.

On impulse, he checked the rear door. It was locked.

Taking a step back, he scanned the windows. None of them looked disturbed.

Should he tell Shelby about this?

Tell her what? That I saw someone walking behind the building to a public parking lot? That not a crime.

Paranoia must seep up out of the ground in Loomis.

Shaking his head, he started back the way he had come. Returning to the front entrance, he climbed the steps reluctantly. This would be his last visit. The less he saw of Shelby Mason before he left town, the better it would be for the both of them.

She was a settle-down, white-picket-fence, church-on-Sunday kind of woman. He was none of those things.

And even if he might want a life like that someday, it wouldn't be here.

At five minutes before eight, the mayor and the five library board members were already gathered in the small meeting room adjacent to the area where Shelby and Wendy held story time. Charla had arrived a few moments before. Tonight she was minus her dog, but she had her driver, Bosworth, attending her.

Wendy was busy offering refreshments and visiting with the group. From the doorway, Shelby heard her ask the mayor point-blank if the Mother's Day Festival was being canceled. He assured her it was not. His assertion that this year's event was going to be the biggest and most successful ever rang slightly hollow.

Their conversation gave Shelby a few more minutes to compose herself. She had rehearsed her presentation a number of times, but she went over it once more. It had to be perfect. So much was riding on it.

Pressing her hands together, she paced behind the counter.

"We would welcome the chance. No, we welcome the opportunity to develop a collection dedicated to identifying and promoting research into the history and peoples of Loomis, St. Tammany Parish and all of Louisiana."

She bit her thumbnail. Did that sound too pretentious?

Dropping her hand, she continued. "By actively seeking out and preserving books, maps and manuscripts at our library, we could provide the residents of Loomis with a unique glimpse into their history. Such a center would also attract to our town visitors seeking genealogy information. Visitors who would improve our local economy by increased tourism spending."

The sound of clapping made her whirl around. Patrick stood just inside the doorway, watching her. "The tourism spending part is a good touch."

At the sight of his crooked smile, her nervous butterflies settled. A warm glow of happiness filled her. He was here. She had at least one more chance to spend time with him before he left town.

"You don't think it's too much?"

He walked forward. "No, it sounds great."

Looking down, she acknowledged that his simple presence made her heart race, but nothing about her tangled emotions were simple. She liked this man way too much for her own good.

It was time to let her rational mind steer her heart, not the other way around.

So much stood between them. His lack of faith, his disdain for the town and the people she loved. Plus, he'd soon be riding off into the sunset without a backward glance.

Allowing herself to become more involved was a sure path to heartbreak.

Keep it casual, Shelby Sue. Be smart.

"Thanks for the kind words. What brings you in so late?" She busied herself with gathering together various pieces of paper scattered across the countertop.

"I knew it was your big night." He pushed a package wrapped in plain brown paper across the counter toward her.

"What is this?" Reaching out, she drew it close.

"Open it and see."

Slipping a finger beneath the corner of the paper, she carefully pried up the tape. "I love getting presents. Did someone tell you that?"

"I made a wild guess."

Pulling aside the wrapping, she stared at the *Memoirs of Sadie Winslow* and two of the journals dated from before the Civil War.

"Patrick, these are some of the most valuable books in your mother's collection. Are you sure you want to do this?"

"First, you pester me for them, and now you're not sure you want to accept them? Woman, make up your mind."

Smiling, Shelby clutched them to her chest. "I do want them. Thank you so much. I'll get you a receipt as soon as I have them appraised."

"No receipt. They're for you, not for the library. If you want to start a research center with them, that's up to you."

Sighing, she said, "I don't know how to thank you." Sudden tears threatened. Remaining casual had never been so hard.

Just then Wendy came hurrying down the aisle toward them. "Shelby, they'll be ready for y'all in a few minutes. I think everyone is settled."

Holding up the books, Shelby forced herself to smile at her cousin. "Look what Patrick gave us."

"Gave you," he corrected.

"Gave me, and I'm donating them to the Dylan Renault Research Center for Loomis History and Genealogy."

"Which we won't have unless you get in that room and wow the old battle-ax."

"Wendy!" Shelby tried to sound appalled but barely managed to suppress a chuckle.

"I know, I'm sorry. Come wow our potentially magnanimous benefactor."

"All right." Stepping through the gate in the counter, Shelby paused to glance at Patrick. "You're welcome to come to the meeting. It is open to the public, although guests are rare."

She made the offer but didn't expect him to accept. He wasn't a boardroom-meeting kind of guy.

"I really should get going."

"Of course. Thanks again for these." She patted the books she still clutched. "They'll be wonderful additions to our library even if we don't get Mrs. Renault's money. Goodbye, Mr. Rivers."

"I liked it better when you called me Patrick," he said, and smiled.

Would she see him again? Gripping her lower lip between her teeth, Shelby turned away to follow Wendy.

When they were out of Patrick's earshot, Wendy leaned close. "Men as handsome and dangerous as that one should have to wear big yellow caution signs 'round their necks."

"That only helps if you're smart enough to read the sign."

"True. I wish he'd go away before he breaks your heart."

Tears stung Shelby's eyes at the deep concern on her cousin's face. "My heart's okay, but thank you for caring."

The door to the meeting room opened and Mrs. Carmichael, the library chairperson, came out. "I'm excited about your proposal, Miss Mason. I do hope Charla is as well. I'll be right back, ladies."

"Oh, great," Wendy muttered. "He's coming this way again."

Shelby turned to see Patrick walking toward them.

He grinned at Wendy's sour stare. "I've changed my mind. I think I'll stay for the meeting after all."

Sniffing once, Shelby decided a quick side trip to the ladies' room was in order for her, too. She needed a little more time to compose herself and to splash some cold water on her heated face. Pleading her case coherently with both Mrs. Renault and Patrick in the room would take a lot of poise.

Please, Lord, let me do this right.

Starting toward the ladies' room, she was startled when the door flew open and Mrs. Carmichael burst out. "Someone call the police! There's been a break-in!"

Holding open the door to the restroom, she gestured inside. The tall, narrow window stood open. A message was scrawled in peach lipstick across the oval mirror above the sinks.

I'm watching you, Shelzie. I'll know if you talk.

EIGHT

"It's a simple case of vandalism. I don't know what the fuss is about. The police should be concentrating on my son's murder, not wasting time investigating a harmless prank." Mrs. Renault folded her hands in her lap and gave Deputy Olson a pointed glare.

"I don't think the pranks were meant to be harmless." Patrick had only to look at Shelby's face to realize how upset and frightened she was.

The group was seated around a conference table in the meeting room. Two deputies had made a sweep of the building but found nothing unusual. One had gone outside to check the grounds while Deputy Olson took everyone's statements.

Mrs. Carmichael shivered. "To think, he was right in there. He could have attacked any one of us."

Shelby rubbed her hands up and down her arms. "Or she. One of the children called me Shelzie. Sarah corrected him. Someone who was here that day wrote this note."

Patrick wanted to reach out and gather her close. Against his better judgment he wanted to hold her, take away her fear, protect her. "Who might have overheard that remark?"

"You, Wendy, Mrs. Renault, at least a dozen women and

their children. Wendell Bixby's sister and his niece were there. So was your granddaughter, Mr. Mayor. Barb Tibbs and her boys, I don't know who else."

"Was there anyone you didn't know in the group?" the deputy asked.

Shelby bit her fingernail as she shook her head, then looked at Wendy.

Her cousin shrugged. "There was one new woman with two kids. I don't know her name. I don't know who else was in the building at the time. I really wasn't paying attention. I do remember opening the window because it was such a nice morning. Someone lurking outside could have over-heard the children."

Charla turned her wheelchair to face the officer. "This is going nowhere. I don't see why I'm being detained. I'd like to go now."

"I have a few more questions." Deputy Olson consulted the notebook in his hand.

"It looks as if whoever did this came in through the window. The screen is lying on the ground outside. It would help if we could narrow down the time it happened. Miss Mason, when was the last time anyone used the room?"

"I can't be sure. I was in there about seven o'clock because a patron told me the sink was stopped up."

"And the window was closed then?"

"Yes, I'm sure of it."

"Were any of you ladies in there after that time?"

Wendy held up her hand. "I went in about a quarter to eight. I know the window was closed, and there was nothing on the mirror." Leaning forward, Wendy asked, "Mrs. Renault, didn't I see you go in after that?"

"I did. I don't recall if the window was open, but there wasn't any writing on the mirror."

The deputy jotted a note. "What time was that?"

Charla lifted one shoulder in an indifferent shrug. "Perhaps seven-fifty."

"That's about when I saw someone lurking at the back of the building," Patrick interjected. "I checked the back door and it was locked. None of the windows were open."

Charla raised an eyebrow. "So you say, Mr. Rivers. A good way to explain your fingerprints at the scene. We have only your word that you saw someone. These *episodes* at the library all began after *you* arrived in town."

He smiled without warmth. "The only evidence I can offer in my defense is that peach lipstick isn't really my shade. Is it yours?"

The Renault matriarch's mouth flew open, then snapped shut. "Well, I never!"

It was plain her preferred shade was deep crimson, but Patrick couldn't resist taunting her.

Mrs. Carmichael said, "It looked like the same shade you're wearing, Miss Mason. It's not pink, it's more apricot. It's most becoming. I know how hard it is to find a good shade when you have red hair." Her voice trailed off.

"There!" Charla announced. "Miss Mason could have written the note herself in a pathetic attempt to gain attention."

"I did not!" Shelby shot back.

"Okay, folks," the mayor quickly intervened. "Let's not get into an argument. It appears nothing was stolen or damaged. All we have is a little graffiti that can be easily removed and a broken window screen."

Deputy Olson rubbed the side of his nose. "Do you have your lipstick with you, Miss Mason?"

Patrick moved to stand behind Shelby and place a comforting hand on her shoulder. "This is nuts. This woman is the victim."

Shelby patted his hand. "It's all right. My lipstick is in my purse. The police are welcome to check it against the message on the mirror. I have nothing to hide. I'll get it."

Watching her leave the room, Patrick's anger grew. Why would anyone think Shelby would do something like this? Even as the question formed in his mind, he had an answer. Because it was easier to believe the worst of people than it was to trust them.

He knew how hard it was to prove yourself innocent when the police were looking for easy answers.

Wendy, her hand clasped in front of her on the table, said, "Shelby's lipstick is a common brand sold at several places in town. Even if it matches, it won't prove anything except the person doing this is observant."

Shelby returned a few moments later and handed the deputy a silver tube.

He took it and closed his notebook. "Thank you. I'm going to file a report, but there isn't much we can do. We'll dust for fingerprints, check for footprints outside and run this lipstick to see if it's a match."

Glaring at the man, Patrick blurted out, "This is the third threat aimed at Miss Mason. I think your office should be more concerned that she has a stalker, in light of recent events in this town."

"I believe I've wasted enough time here tonight," Charla declared. She gestured to her driver standing motionless at the rear of the room. "Bosworth, bring the car around."

Bosworth nodded and strode from the room.

The mayor became instantly solicitous. "This has been a most unfortunate event. We will reschedule Miss Mason's presentation at a time that will be convenient for you, Mrs. Renault."

"Don't bother. I believe my money will be better spent

elsewhere." Pushing forward the small joystick on the arm of her chair, Charla wheeled herself out of the room.

Shelby barely heard Mrs. Renault's pronouncement. The library expansion hardly seemed important now.

Someone was watching her. Someone had overheard the childish mispronunciation of Shelby's name. The thought made Shelby's blood run cold.

With a sharp intake of breath, she pressed a hand to her lips.

There had already been one kidnapping attempt on Sarah. Was this somehow related? The FBI had proven that Angelina Loring had been behind that attempt, but she was dead. Her accomplice was in jail.

Who was spying on Shelby and Sarah now? Another accomplice the police didn't know about? Was Sarah safe?

Shelby turned and raced to the checkout counter. She grabbed the phone and quickly punched in Clint's number. He answered on the third ring.

"Clint, this is Shelby. Where is Sarah?"

"She's in bed asleep. Why?"

"Go check on her right now."

"Shelby, you're scaring me."

"Just do it. I'll explain when you come back to the phone."

The receiver clattered as Clint dropped it.

The minutes seem to stretch on forever. Shelby chewed on her fingernail. Finally, she heard him pick up the phone again.

"Sarah's fine. She's asleep."

"Oh, thank the Lord." Relief made her weak in the knees.

"Mind telling me why I broke the land speed record getting up my stairs?"

"Someone broke into the library tonight and scrawled a threatening note on the mirror. Someone has been watching

Sarah and me together. I just needed to be sure she was safe and make you aware of this."

"Sarah is fine, but what about you?"

"I'll be okay. It's some kind of prank."

"Like the snake? These pranks are getting too frequent for my liking, Shelby. You be careful."

"I will. Thanks, Clint. I'll talk to you later." She hung up and found Wendy and Patrick waiting for her.

He leaned his forearms on the counter. "I'm sorry I antagonized the old battle-ax, but she acts like the world revolves around her and no one else is important."

"That's okay." The badly needed funds for the library had vanished like dissipating smoke. Shelby wasn't sure her spirits could get much lower.

The mayor, accompanied by the other members of the library board, filed out. Mrs. Carmichael stopped for a moment at the counter. "Perhaps Charla can be persuaded to change her mind about hearing your proposal. I'll speak to her tomorrow before church services. Will I see you there?"

Shelby nodded. "Of course. As for Mrs. Renault, she's not going to change her mind. I don't think she really wanted us to have the money in the first place." Shelby swallowed her disappointment.

"Don't give up so easily, Shelby." Patrick's words brought her head up. She looked into his eyes, brimming with understanding and encouragement.

"You're right. Mrs. Carmichael, I'll speak to Mrs. Renault myself. This project is my idea, and it's a good one for the community. I can make her see that."

"All right, my dear." Mrs. Carmichael smiled slightly, then walked to the door where the mayor was waiting for her.

Stepping behind the desk, Wendy picked up her purse. "I think you should come home with me, Shelby."

"Thanks, but I'm fine. I'll be even better when I'm in my own bed."

"You're sure?"

"Absolutely."

Wendy turned to Patrick. "Thanks for speaking up for Shelby back there. I was kinda hoping peach *was* the old battle-ax's color."

Patrick grinned. "Unfortunately, the writing was higher than she could have reached from her wheelchair."

"Yeah, I thought of that. I hope the police catch who did it, but I'm not holding my breath. Be sure and lock your doors and windows tonight, Shelby Sue."

"I will. You do the same."

As her cousin left, Shelby gathered her bag and stepped out from behind the counter. "You don't have to stick around. It won't take me a minute to lock up."

"I'm sticking around until you're finished here, then I'm taking you home." Patrick draped an arm around Shelby's shoulders.

His warmth, the leather-and-spicy scent of him, his strength, all served to bring her comfort. She soaked it in like a sponge. "I'm all right."

"Nevertheless, I'm still taking you home."

"On your bike?"

"I know you've been dying to get a ride on it since the day I pulled into town."

If he was trying to make her smile, he succeeded. "Busted. But my car is in the parking lot. If you'll walk me that far, I can get home by myself." Would she be safe even there?

"Okay, but this may be the only offer of a ride you're gonna get from me."

Together, they walked out of the library. Shelby locked the door while Patrick waited on the steps.

She really thought she was fine until she saw how far away she had parked. Her car was at the very back corner of the lot. The fog had moved in, carrying with it the damp, decaying smell of the bayou. The streetlamps barely penetrated the darkness.

She couldn't count the number of times she'd crossed this lot without a second of worry. After Leah's disappearance and Dylan and Angelina's murders, she had been cautious and watchful of her surroundings, but not fearful.

Tonight, even with Patrick at her side, she couldn't force herself to walk back there. The deep shadows of the buildings that bordered the lot offered too many hiding places.

Someone was watching her.

A surge of fear flooded her brain, causing her heart to hammer against her chest. She licked suddenly dry lips.

"Are you okay?" Patrick's quiet query made her realize just how frightened she was.

"No, I'm not okay."

He took her into his arms. "When I find out who is doing this, I'm going to beat him to a pulp."

She wanted to burrow beneath his skin. Inside the circle of his arms, she felt safe. "I wish I was as strong and brave as you are."

"I might have a little more muscle, but I don't have the corner on brave."

"Between the two of us, you're winning hands down."

"Come on, I'll take you home."

"Thank you." She was grateful that he left his arm across her shoulders as they walked to his bike. In spite of the warm muggy air, she still shivered.

When they reached his motorcycle, he detached himself long enough to hand her his helmet. Slipping it on, she waited as he adjusted the strap and tightened it beneath her chin. She glanced around the quiet street.

He rapped his knuckles on top of the helmet. "Feeling safer?"

"Not particularly. Do I look as fashion-challenged as I feel?"

"No, you look cute."

Her spirits lifted. "Really?"

Chuckling, he straddled the bike, and she slipped onto the seat behind him. Wrapping her arms tightly around his chest, she pressed herself against his back.

He patted her hands. "Breathing is still a requirement for me."

"Sorry." Loosening her grip, she made herself relax.

"Where would you like to go?" he asked over his shoulder.

She checked the street again. Was there someone standing beneath the trees across the road? "L.A. sounds good."

"Where would you like me to take you tonight?" The amusement in his tone helped her regain her composure.

"Home, I guess."

"Are you sure you shouldn't go to Wendy's?" .

For a second she considered giving him Wendy's address, but stopped herself. What if she brought danger to their door? Wendy had a husband and children. Shelby would never forgive herself if something happened to them because of her.

"Can we just ride around for a while?"

"Sure. Are you scared to go home?"

"A little." She didn't want to be afraid.

Lord, help me. Give me courage. Don't let me give in to the fear.

"I'll check your place out from top to bottom before I leave. How's that?"

"You've got a deal."

"Okay, hold on."

She didn't need to be told twice. Despite all her misgivings, it was exactly what she wanted to do.

NINE

Shelby pressed her cheek to Patrick's back as they traveled through town. He hadn't worn his leather jacket tonight. She could feel the warmth of his skin through the fabric of his shirt. With her arms around his waist, she couldn't help but notice the taut muscles of his abdomen. The erratic pace of her heart made her all too aware of him as a man.

If only he would stay. I could go on holding him like this forever.

Even as she thought about a future that included him, she had to discard it. He would never stay in Loomis. And he'd turn his back on God.

Her long hair hung out from under the helmet and twisted into tangles as it blew behind her. It would take longer than usual to brush it when she got home. Much longer.

Home. It was only a few blocks away. When they got there, she'd have to let go of him. She didn't want to do that. As silly as she knew the desire was, she wanted to rest against him for a long, long time.

When they rolled to a stop at a red light, he turned his head. "Are you hungry?"

She had been too nervous about her presentation to bother with supper. "I'm starving."

"Where's a good place to eat at this time of night?"

"Bitsy's Diner is still open." It was the closest place she could think of.

"Is that good Cajun place still in business between here and Lacombe?"

"Do you mean the Creole Kitchen?"

"That's the one. They used to serve killer seafood gumbo."

"They still do."

The light had changed. A car pulled up behind them and honked.

"Are you sure you're up for a road trip?" he asked.

She could just see the corner of his smile. "Absolutely."

"That's my girl." Gunning the engine, he sped through the intersection. Within minutes, the lights of the city fell behind them.

The highway ran straight as an arrow past small farms and occasional clusters of houses. Patrick's large, powerful machine ate up the miles as it roared through the darkness. Fifteen minutes later, they reached the edge of Fontainebleau State Park. After that, there was only the dense forest pressing close to the road and the occasional headlights of an oncoming car.

The ride was glorious. Even with her face pressed against Patrick's broad back, the wind still brought tears to her eyes. All she could hear was the rush of the air blowing past her ears and the roar of the engine as they sailed along the road. Now she understood why he loved it.

All too soon, they left the forest behind and Patrick slowed to turn into a crowded parking lot just off the highway. He pulled up to the front of the building and stopped beside several other motorcycles.

The sounds of laughter and Cajun music poured out the open doorway of the converted barn, along with the rich aromas of the restaurant's famous cooking.

Stepping off the bike, Shelby pulled her helmet from her head and shook out her hair. Patrick took the helmet from her and hung it over the handlebar. Two men dressed in black leather vests and leather pants walked out of the diner and strolled past.

"Nice bike," the first one said, nodding to Patrick.

"Nice back warmer, too." The younger blond guy winked at Shelby. She took a step closer to Patrick.

"Pay him no mind, miss," his buddy said. Tipping his head to one side, he took a longer look at the bike. "Who designed it for you?"

"I did."

"No joke? Who built it?"

"Carl Wolf."

"Wolfwind Cycles out of L.A.? I've heard of them." He held out his hand. "Name's Ben Cooper."

Patrick shook his hand. "Patrick Rivers. This is Shelby Mason."

"Rivers? I know that name."

Shelby felt Patrick tense.

Ben grinned, showing a gap-toothed smile. "You're the fella that won the International Motorcycle Design Award last December in Phoenix. I read about you in *Custom Cycles* magazine. That was one sweet ride you built."

"Thanks."

"It's an honor to meet you, man."

As the two men walked away, Shelby turned to Patrick. "You're famous?"

He shook his head. "I wouldn't go that far."

"International Motorcycle Design Award–winner. I'm impressed."

"I'm hungry." He motioned toward the door. "Let's eat before they close."

Inside the building, they were shown to a booth in the corner, away from the band and the couples gliding around the small dance floor. The rough wooden beams of the converted barn were decorated with strings of tiny lights. In the bright atmosphere, it was easy to push aside the frightening event of the evening.

Sliding into the high-backed wooden bench, Shelby propped her hands on the red-checkered vinyl tablecloth and leaned toward Patrick. "I have to ask. What's a back warmer?"

"A biker term for the chick riding behind him."

"Oh, well, that makes sense. I never thought of myself as a biker chick."

"I've never thought of you that way, either."

"I did enjoy the ride. It was exhilarating."

"I'm glad."

The way he stared at her sent a wave of heat to her face. She looked down and pulled her tangled hair over her shoulder. Twisting it into a rope, she had a chance to compose herself.

This is only the kind gesture of a friend. Don't read more into it.

Fortunately, the waitress arrived to take their order. When she left, Patrick leaned back in the booth and propped one arm around the back of the bench. "Mrs. Carmichael said she'll see you at church tomorrow. Tomorrow's Friday. Is someone getting married or something?"

She frowned. Did he really not know what day it was? "Tomorrow is Good Friday."

"Oh, sure. I don't pay much attention to holidays. I guess I lost track."

"That's a shame. The day Jesus Christ died on the cross for our sins is a day that should never be forgotten."

"Is this the you-should-get-religion speech?"

"No. This is the *I-have-religion speech,* and I don't want you poking fun at me for my beliefs."

"Whoa, Miss Shelby is getting spunky."

"Having your name scrawled on a mirror in lipstick tends to do that to people."

"Who do you think did it?"

"I don't know."

"You don't have any idea who'd want to frighten you?"

"Well, Chuck Peters has been acting very strange toward me lately."

"Chuck Peters. Is he a jilted boyfriend?"

"Hardly. I'm sure you've seen him around. He's the homeless man, small, with thin red hair. He's a very sad case. He drinks heavily, and he's had some psychiatric problems in the past."

"He sounds like a perfect candidate for a stalker."

"I'm not so sure."

"Why? Because you feel sorry for him?"

"It's not that. The timing, the physical skill to climb in the window—it just seems more complex than Chuck could manage."

"Maybe his drunkenness is an act. Maybe he's crazy like a fox."

"Maybe." She paused as she considered how much she should say about Coral's visit.

He leaned closer. "What?"

"Nothing."

His eyes narrowed. "No, you have something you want to share."

"What makes you say that?"

"When I told you I could read your face like a book, I wasn't kidding."

"Like a *first-grade* book."

"That rankled, did it?" A grin tugged at the corner of his mouth.

"I never thought of myself as so transparent."

"It's your best quality, Shelby. Don't ever lose it."

As compliments went, it was one of the nicest she'd ever received. Stunned, she could only shake her head. "I never know what you're going to say."

"Unpredictability. *My* best quality. So what were *you* going to say?"

"Coral Travis came to see me today."

"Ah, another snake in the library. You're gonna have to start calling it the Loomis Reptile House."

"I know you harbor a lot of animosity toward her—"

"*Ya think?*"

His hostility almost silenced Shelby, but she decided to plow ahead. "I think she's put herself in a position she doesn't know how to get out of. Social status has always been her brass ring. She's engaged to an up-and-coming politician, with her sights set far beyond being Mrs. Mayor. She has a lot to protect."

"Wait a minute. You're saying Coral Travis is behind the threats?"

"The first note I got said to keep my fat mouth shut. Coral used to make fun of me because I was an overweight teenager."

"I can't see Coral climbing through a window, and I *really* can't see her touching a snake unless she's changed a lot in the last ten years. Besides, why threaten you?"

"Ten years ago, when I was still practicing being invisible, I was at the after-game party the night our team won the championship."

"So was most of the university. It was the biggest bonfire that part of the bayou had seen in a while."

"I overheard Coral talking to someone. They were just out of sight in the trees."

"Who?"

"I'm not sure, but I think it was a man. I plainly heard her say she was going home with the football hero whether he knew it or not. She wasn't going to settle for second string. She was talking about *you,* Patrick. *You* were going places and she was going along. She saw me there. A little while later, I saw you kissing her and I knew she was going to get what she wanted. After that, I left."

What she didn't share was how seeing that kiss made her feel—totally insignificant. In that moment, she knew her day-dreams about catching Patrick Rivers's attention and winning his affection were baseless. In a sad way, she had grown up that night.

A shuttered look descended over his face. He didn't say anything.

The waitress arrived a few moments later with their order. Shelby inhaled the mouthwatering aroma, then busied herself stirring the piping hot gumbo. Lifting a spoonful to her mouth, she blew the steam away.

"I thought it was my idea," Patrick said softly. He was looking down at his bowl, but she could see he was focused in the past. "That tells you how conceited I was back then. A few beers and I was eager to get her alone. She told me her roommate was out of town and we could go there. We made love. I talked about my plans to design motorcycles. She had some silly notion that I was going to play pro football. I think I even laughed at the idea. Anyway, you know the rest."

Shelby's appetite fled. She didn't want to hear the details of his night with Coral. Stirring her soup, she tried to get the vision of them together out of her mind. To no avail.

She put her spoon down. "After you were arrested, I wanted to tell someone what I heard, but I never did. When you were released, I thought it wouldn't make any difference."

"It wouldn't have. It would still have been her word against mine. There were no witnesses. No one even saw us leave the party together."

"But if I had spoken up about what Coral said—maybe people wouldn't have been so quick to believe her. I'm sorry."

Patrick raked a hand through his hair and leaned back. "It's water under the bridge, Shelby."

Was he really going to let her off the hook that easily? His whole life had hit the skids in part because she didn't speak up to defend him.

Would it have made any difference? Maybe not, but just maybe he could have salvaged his relationship with his stepfather or with his friend Wyatt.

"I know it doesn't change anything, but I wanted you to know." She looked ready to burst into tears.

"It's okay." To his surprise, he wasn't angry with her.

They had both been so young. He couldn't expect a painfully shy young woman like she'd been back then to stick up for him when even his own stepfather hadn't.

His bitterness and anger had sustained him for a long time. Those emotions had driven him to succeed, sabotaged his relationships with any woman who cared about him, left him with nothing but his work. He thought he wanted it that way.

But it wasn't enough anymore. He wanted more out of his life. He wanted it to mean something. He didn't know where to start, but he suspected the answer might be found, in part, with Miss Shelby Mason.

"So you think Coral Travis is behind your threats?"

He picked up his spoon and began to eat the rich seafood

gumbo. The spices heated up his mouth and made him grab for his glass of water. He'd forgotten how fiery-good real Cajun food could be.

"I really don't know what to think. I'm not sure if I'd rather believe someone I know did it or that a stranger is fixated on me. Both are creepy thoughts."

"We'll have to hope the police come up with some evidence."

"I can't help wondering if this is somehow related to Leah's disappearance and the other murders, but I just don't see how. I keep racking my brain and coming up empty."

"Then focus on something else."

"Like what?"

"Your new Easter bonnet. I'll bet it's green with yellow daisies around the brim."

She chuckled. It was a good sound. He could hear it for the rest of his life. The thought startled him. It was impossible, of course, but it didn't keep him from wanting it.

"I don't have an Easter bonnet, but I did get a new dress."

Determined to lighten things up, he wagged a finger at her. "It's green with yellow daisies, isn't it?"

"No."

"Okay, what color is it?"

Raising her chin, she tilted her head ever so slightly. "I'm not going to tell you. If you want to see it, come to church on Sunday."

So the little pixie thought she could handle him. He kept a straight face with some difficulty. "You think I won't?"

That made her look at him closely. "Would you? Not because I was teasing you, of course, but because…it's the right thing to do."

"Why not? The good folks of Loomis deserve one more shock before I leave town."

Sighing heavily, she replied, "That's not quite the right attitude."

"If God wants me in church, He'll have to take me attitude and all."

"At least you're being honest about it."

No, he wasn't. He was angling to spend more time with her. Had he really sunk that low? "Never mind."

Looking down, she stirred her gumbo slowly. "We could go together if you'd rather not go alone."

TEN

"Well? What did he say?" Wendy demanded.

Shelby cautiously opened the lid of the return book bin and peeked in. Nothing sprang, crawled or slid out. Nothing ominous moved within. She propped the lid open and began removing the items inside. "He said *yes*."

"Y'all are joking." Wendy took the books, videos and audiobooks Shelby handed her and sorted them on a small, tan metal cart.

Shelby closed the lid and faced her cousin. "Not joking a bit."

"You're actually going to church with Patrick Rivers on Easter Sunday."

"Why are you so shocked? Even you've taken a liking to him."

"I'll admit he's good-looking in a bad boy sort of way." She gestured toward the locked display case where Shelby showcased the journals he'd given her. "Giving you those books was a very nice touch. It's also hard not to like a guy who stands up to Charla Renault. Of course, he doesn't have to live in this town."

Shelby propped her hands on her hips. "I don't think that would make a difference to him. He doesn't much care what people think of him."

"You really think Coral lied about that night?"

"I do. I wish there was some way to prove it." Shelby moved to the computer to begin scanning the returns back into the system.

"Don't hold your breath waiting for Coral's conscience to kick in."

"I won't hold my breath, but I'll pray she does the right thing."

Wendy finished loading her cart with books waiting to be reshelved. "Can't go wrong with praying for someone."

Shelby glanced at the cloudy gray skies beyond the window overlooking the drive-up lane. "Sometimes prayer isn't enough. Sometimes we have to act. My heart tells me this is one of those times." She pounded her fist into her palm. "I have to *do* something."

"Wow. Hanging around Patrick is having quite an effect on y'all."

Embarrassment flooded Shelby. She knew her face must be beet-red. "I don't know what you mean."

"Don't get me wrong. You're as sweet as they come, but it's not like you to go charging in where angels fear to tread."

"You make me sound like an Amazon warrior. I assure you I'm not."

"Bayou warrior. That has a better ring to it. Honestly, Shelby, you've already spoken to Coral. What else can you do?"

"I'm going to call Jocelyn and see what she thinks. She and Ava Renault are good friends. Maybe Jocelyn can give me some insight on how to proceed."

"That's sort of her job. Are you really going to go see Charla Renault, too?"

"I am," Shelby declared with fresh determination. "First thing tomorrow morning."

"Confronting the dragon in her den. I don't know, Shelby, I'm thinking she's gonna barbecue you for lunch."

Shelby rolled her eyes at her cousin. "Could you sound a little more encouraging?"

Wendy shook her head. "No."

"Fine. If I get her to change her mind, you have to buy me breakfast on Monday."

"You've got a deal."

"You'll see. I can be very persuasive when I set my mind to something." Shelby turned to smile at the man waiting at the counter to check out a stack of books.

Pushing the cart past her, Wendy leaned in to whisper, "I'm not sure there's a single person in all of Louisiana who can get Ms. Charla to change her mind."

"You piece of junk! Give it up!" Squatting on the garage floor on Saturday afternoon, Patrick wrestled with an awkwardly placed bolt on his bike. He'd pay more attention to the mechanic's needs with his next design.

"What's the matter with her?"

Raising his head, Patrick was surprised to see Wyatt standing just inside the open shop door. It was the first overture his former friend had made.

"She's leaking oil. I think I have a cracked gasket."

"Need a hand?" Wyatt's hesitant offer made it plain he expected Patrick to refuse. As an olive branch it wasn't much, but it was a start.

"Sure. See if you can keep this wrench on the bolt while I loosen the nut with my ratchet."

Taking the tool Patrick held out to him, Wyatt crouched on the opposite side of the bike and affixed the wrench. "Okay."

Now able to pull down on the handle with both hands, Patrick loosened the nut easily.

"Thanks." Patrick arranged himself cross-legged on the cement floor and looked at Wyatt still squatting on the other side. So much unsaid, so much to say. Where could they start?

Lord, help me heal this rift. I miss my friend.

Had he just uttered a prayer? Shelby had to be rubbing off on him. Wyatt ran his hand over the black leather seat and said, "She's a beauty."

There was genuine admiration in his tone.

Patrick allowed himself a touch of professional pride. "Thanks."

"So how long does it take to make something like this?"

"It depends. If the whole crew is working on it, a week."

"No way!"

"Sometimes the design work actually takes longer than the production."

"I came over to say thanks for giving me the present your mom got me. You didn't have to do that."

Patrick allowed himself a little smile. Shelby had been right. "Mom would have wanted you to have it."

"She was a great lady."

"Yes, she was. Shelby Mason was the one who found them. She was looking through some of my mother's books and came across one for you and one for me. I got *The Adventures of Tom Sawyer*. What did you get?"

"My Side of the Mountain."

"Man, I haven't thought about that story in years. Remember the big hollow tree that boy lived in? It was a great story."

Recalling one of his favorite childhood books made Patrick smile.

Wyatt nodded in agreement. "Fishing, hunting, taming wild animals for friends, it was the perfect life for a kid."

"It reminds me of the time we spent out at your family's cabin on the bayou."

Standing, Wyatt shoved his hands in the front pocket of his faded jeans. "You like it in California, don't you? I mean… you wouldn't be building a beauty like this if you'd stayed here."

Patrick wondered why the sudden change in the conversation. "L.A. is okay."

"So it was a good thing you moved away."

Perhaps on some level it had been, but he could have done without the jump start of Coral's accusations.

Let it go. It's in the past.

"What about you, Wyatt? You had big plans. You were going to start your own car repair business. Did that work out?"

"Big dreams take money, which I didn't have."

"I always wondered how it turned out for you. I wrote to my dad, but he never wrote back. I used to wonder what Coral did after—"

For a long moment, Wyatt didn't say anything and Patrick thought he'd pressed the issue too soon.

Wyatt answered slowly. "I hear she has her sights set on marrying the next mayor. Did you know I asked her out once? She wasn't interested in a second string guy like me."

"You were never second string, Wyatt. You were a great player."

"Kinda sad if you think about it. The high point of my life was a football field in college."

"You're married, you have kids. That has to be a bigger high than our championship win."

"Yeah, you're right. I dropped out of school the next year and went to work at the mill like my dad. I met Barb two years later, and we got married."

"She seems nice."

"She's a better woman than I deserve."

"So, she's the reason you stayed in town?"

Wyatt nodded. "She didn't like the idea of moving away from her friends and her family. My folks wanted to retire to Arizona, so I bought the place from them. The boys came along bang bang and the time to leave never did. I envy you, Pat."

"Envy *me?* Why?" Patrick couldn't hide his surprise.

"You've got nothing to tie you down. You've got the freedom of the open road at your fingertips. You can go anywhere, do anything."

Patrick rose to his feet and moved to replace his stepfather's ratchet in a tool chest he'd found on a workbench at the rear of the building. "The open road thing is overrated, Wyatt."

"Is it? I wonder. Have you talked to her?"

"Who?"

"Coral."

Patrick concentrated on closing the lid of the chest without slamming it. "We've spoken."

"I thought maybe the two of you could find a way to let bygones be bygones."

"She accused me of rape. I'd still be in prison if she'd been able to make the charges stick."

"It wouldn't have gone that far."

"Wouldn't it?" Patrick looked over his shoulder.

Wyatt was staring at the wrench in his hand. "I don't think Coral would have let it go to trial."

Walking back to the bike, Patrick held out his hand for the tool. "I really wish it had."

Wyatt looked surprised. "Why?"

"Because then I'd have had a chance to defend myself in front of everyone."

"The charges were dropped."

"Believe me, that's not the same thing as being found innocent. You don't know what it's like having everyone believe you raped a woman and got away with it. Even my best friend didn't speak up for me."

Wyatt placed the wrench in Patrick's outstretched hand. "What if that friend regretted his actions?"

Patrick had waited for an explanation for so many years. Now, he was almost afraid to hear it. "I guess the best thing would be to tell me why."

"I was in love with Coral."

It wasn't what Patrick expected to hear. Almost every guy on the football team had had a thing for Coral, but he never knew Wyatt's feeling for her had been so strong.

Patrick carried the wrench to the tool chest and laid it inside. As he closed the lid, he acknowledged he'd been more than stupid that night. He'd been blind as well.

"I'm really sorry, Wyatt. I didn't know I was betraying my best friend."

He turned around, but Wyatt was gone.

ELEVEN

"You didn't bring the bike?"

Standing beside him on the walk in front of her house, Patrick saw Shelby scowl at the dark-blue sedan parked at the curb.

Cocking his head to one side, he studied the cute pout on her disappointed features. "I rented a car for the day because I thought you'd be more comfortable wearing your Easter finery in this than on the back of my cycle."

"That's very sweet, but arriving at church on the back of a bike would be the boldest thing I've ever done in my life."

"I doubt that."

"Would I lie to you on Easter Sunday?"

"I hope not. By the way, that dress is very pretty on you."

She twirled around once, letting the full skirt flair out. "Thank you."

"However, it is green."

She looked down. "I'd call it jade, and there isn't a single daisy on it."

"True. Now that I've seen it, I guess I can go home."

Her features settled into a puzzled frown as if she couldn't tell if he was kidding or not.

"You can, if that's what you want to do. I'm not going to stop you."

He really shouldn't tease her. She was far too gullible. "I'm going to church with you, don't worry. Do you always get your way?"

"Not usually. This is a nice change after yesterday afternoon."

"What happened yesterday?"

"I tried to see Charla Renault, but her servant, Bosworth, wouldn't let me in the door."

"Are you giving up?"

"Not a chance. She has to come out of the house someday. I'm actually hoping to see her in church this morning. I do wish you'd brought your motorcycle."

"It's got a leaky gasket."

"Is that bad?"

Chuckling, he took her elbow. "Only if you have to special order one from California."

"I looked up your award article online. Nice photo. You looked prestigious."

"Ha! Nobody could have felt more out of place in a suit and tie than I did for that shot."

As far as Shelby was concerned, he looked equally good in his leather jacket or a three-piece suit. This morning he'd tamed down his biker image by wearing crisp heather-gray slacks with a button-down sage-green shirt.

She could easily find a tie that would go with his outfit. The wifely thought made her smile.

He cocked his head to the side. "What?"

"Nothing." She hoped she wasn't blushing. "What was it like to earn *international* recognition for your work?"

Rolling his eyes, he said, "Tiring. Lots of meetings with motorcycle manufacturing bigwigs from Germany, Japan, England. The best part was the prize money, plus my boss gave me a month's vacation."

His crooked grin and the light in his eyes intrigued her. "Something tells me you didn't spend your vacation cleaning out closets like I did on my last break."

"Closets need to be cleaned? I thought their purpose was to hold stuff."

It was her turn to roll her eyes. "Spoken like a true man. I'm going to guess you took your prize money and blew it in Vegas."

"Wrong. I socked most of it away. The rest I used to take a trip through Mexico."

"On your bike?"

"Is there any other way to travel?"

Wistfully, she said, "You live the most exciting life."

Not at all like the life she led. She glanced at her watch. "I guess we should get going or we'll be late."

Late was good, Patrick thought. Never might be better.

What was he doing going off to worship when he could be working on his bike or getting the house in shape to be sold?

He had a screw loose, that's what was wrong with him.

And Shelby had loosened it.

In going to church, he was begging to get slapped down again by the good folks of Loomis. He knew what it was to be snubbed. Shelby didn't. He swallowed hard. "Maybe this wasn't such a good idea."

"You'll be fine. I promise no one will be thrown to the lions today. Including you."

He returned her smile, but his nervousness intensified.

The trip to the church took only a few minutes. Located just off Main Street, the redbrick structure with its white-trimmed arching windows and steepled bell tower hadn't changed since he was a kid. Behind the church a playground surrounded by a wooden fence marked the boundaries of the Loomis Preschool area.

As Patrick walked through the wide door with Shelby at his side, he was immediately struck by a familiar, long-lost sense of peace.

Sunlight streamed through the stained glass windows. White lilies in large baskets decorated the sanctuary. The rows of wooden pews gleamed with fresh polish. The smell of candle wax and lemon oil was as familiar as the feel of the hard pew where he had squirmed as a boy, wanting to be anywhere but inside on a spring morning.

The sermons back then hadn't meant much to him. He recalled his stepfather hiding his yawns, but not his mother. She paid attention, even through the long-winded ones. For her, Sunday services always held special meanings.

Could he find that meaning for himself? Where would he start?

Glancing around, he noticed only a few people glancing his way. Two pews back and to the right, Coral Travis sat beside her fiancé. There was no mistaking the animosity in her glare or the black scowl on the face of the man beside her. Wendell Bixby looked ready to blow his gasket.

Shelby didn't seem to notice.

She was either good at pretending it didn't bother her or she was still practicing being invisible. Either way, he was sorry he had subjected her to such scrutiny.

A rustle of people turning in their seats made him turn his head as well. Bosworth was wheeling Mrs. Renault to the front of the church.

Charla was resplendent in a suit of robin's egg blue with a matching wide-brimmed hat. Her dog rode in her lap. A small breeze of whispers sifted through the congregation as she passed.

Shelby leaned toward him and he lowered his head to catch her whisper. "At least they aren't talking about you."

Some of the tension drained from his body. "Small favors," he whispered back.

A new rustle of activity began at the rear of the church and spread forward. Unable to keep his curiosity in check, Patrick turned to look.

Lenore Pershing, head held high and wearing a pristine white linen suit and matching hat, walked regally to her place at the front pew opposite Charla.

Patrick saw them exchange daggerlike glances before Lenore took her seat. The breeze of whispers became a small squall inside the church. As he glanced at Shelby for an explanation, he saw even her eyes were wide with shock.

"I can't believe it," she muttered. "Lenore must have gotten out of jail yesterday."

"Jail? What would a Pershing go to jail for in this parish?"

"She tried to keep her son, Max, and Ava Renault apart by making Ava think Max killed Ava's brother, Dylan. The whole thing backfired when the police arrested Max. Lenore finally had to admit what she'd done and was arrested for interfering with a police investigation."

"That's twisted."

"I can't believe she's out already. It isn't right."

Gradually, the whispering around them settled into an uneasy quiet. Turning his attention back to the front of the church Patrick listened to the choir begin the service with joyous song. Before long, he forgot to pay attention to who was looking his way and lost himself in the beat of the music and the message of resurrection.

Reverend Harmon rose and walked to the pulpit. After greeting everyone, he began to talk about salvation and living life anew. They were words that now made sense to Patrick. He wanted a new and different life. He looked down at the woman seated beside him. What would it be like to share a life with her?

Just then, she glanced at him and smiled.

The man who won her heart would be a lucky man indeed.

The service was long, and more than one boy was fidgeting in his pew by the time Reverend Harmon was done, but Patrick wasn't among them. Sitting here was one thing, going outside among the congregation would be the tough part.

At least they all had someone else to talk about today. Maybe Lenore Pershing's arrival was a gift from God to keep the Loomis gossipmongers off his back. He chuckled to himself at the thought that God might be on his side for a change.

As the final note of the choir died away, the parishioners started filing out. Shelby rose, signaling it was time to get on with the inevitable.

The sun was high in the blue sky when Patrick walked out the doors. The Lord had chosen to bless Loomis with a beautiful spring day. To his surprise, Shelby took him by the hand.

"How was it?"

He thought about making some flippant remark, but he couldn't. Her eyes were filled with compassion and hope as she gazed at him.

"It felt good, Shelby. Thank you for inviting me. I've missed talking with God. I didn't realize it until today." He hadn't missed some of the looks cast in his direction but he tried not to let them mar the beauty of the day.

A wide smile wreathed her features. "Great. Come on, there's someone I want you to meet."

After guiding him through the crowd, she stopped beside a tall man with dark eyes and dark hair. The woman at his side had her back to Patrick, but he saw she was a slender woman with strawberry-blond hair.

Shelby stopped in front of the man. "Max, I have someone I'd like to introduce. Max Pershing, this is Patrick Rivers. Patrick, this is Max."

The woman with Max turned to face Patrick. It was Ava Renault.

His heart kicked hard against his ribs, and he readied himself for her scorn.

She maintained the smile on her face with difficulty. Uncertainty clouded her green, almond-shaped eyes.

Patrick considered strangling Shelby on the spot but decided against it. He was just getting back on the Lord's good side.

Shelby looked from Patrick's hard face to Ava's set features and said, "I believe you two know each other."

He nodded toward Ava. "Miss Renault, I was sorry to hear about your brother's death."

"Thank you."

"If you'll excuse us, Shelby and I have to be on our way."

"I don't have anywhere I need to be," Shelby piped up.

What was she trying to prove?

"You don't need to hurry away on my account, Mr. Rivers," Ava said quietly. "Today is a day when Christians should show love and forgiveness to each other as God did to all of us."

"I didn't come here looking for forgiveness."

She tilted her head. "Didn't you? That's odd, because that's exactly what you'll find here."

He glanced around and found Coral glaring at him from across the lawn. "Not everyone feels that way."

"I can't control how others think. I can only ask your forgiveness for myself."

That pulled his attention from Coral back to Ava. "You're asking forgiveness. From me?"

"Shelby, our friend Jocelyn and I had a long conversation last evening. I'm willing to admit I may have been misled by what I saw."

"Misled?"

"Will you accept my apology?" She held out her hand.

He took it more out of reflex than conscious thought. "I don't know what to say."

He released her hand, but she held on. "Say that you can find it in your heart to forgive the wrongs done to you."

Glancing at Shelby, he saw the hopeful look in her eyes. Beyond her, he noticed a number of people staring at them with interest.

With sudden clarity, he knew if Ava Renault and Max Pershing accepted his presence here today, the community was going to view him in a whole new light. It spoke volumes for how much social clout the two families held in the town.

His gaze returned to Ava's face. She knew exactly what she was doing.

Shelby had arranged this. She believed in him. She was willing to stand up for him…and beside him.

Humbled, Patrick nodded. "I accept your apology, Miss Renault."

She smiled brightly and released his fingers.

Max held out his hand. "Shelby told me on the phone yesterday that you're having some problems with a property you want to sell. Something about a missing deed? Maybe I can be of some assistance."

Shelby watched with smug satisfaction as Max and Patrick conferred together. Taking a deep breath, she pressed a hand to her heart and turned to Ava. "Thank you."

"I'll admit I wrestled with my conscience for some time about this last night."

Jocelyn, accompanied by Sam, walked up beside her. "You made the right decision."

"I hope so. Having seen Max falsely accused of murdering my brother has made me see many things in a different light."

Jocelyn reached out and grasped Ava's hand. "That's all behind the two of you now. It's time for wedding plans, Miss Wedding Planner."

Sam scowled. "Lenore Pershing planted evidence to make her son look guilty in your eyes and keep the two of you apart. The justice system isn't always manipulated so easily. And just because Max was innocent doesn't mean Patrick Rivers is. I think I'll run a background check on Mr. Rivers."

Jocelyn wrapped her hands around her husband's arm and squeezed. "Spoken like a true G-man."

Ava folded her arms over her chest as she stared across the lawn at Coral and Wendell getting into their car. "Once I got over the initial shock of finding them together, I had doubts about Coral's story. Something didn't add up. I think that may have been part of the reason we didn't stay friends after that year. But then when Patrick left town so quickly, I thought he *must* be guilty."

Shelby sighed. "That's what a lot of people thought. But Patrick left because he didn't see any way to clear his name."

Sam said, "There's no statute of limitations on rape in Louisiana. Your friend could find himself back in jail if Miss Travis decided to push the issue. In that case, Ava, you could testify only to what you saw and heard. Not what you thought later."

Shelby glanced to where Max and Patrick were still engaged in conversation. "I think he knows that."

Beyond the men, Shelby saw Bosworth helping Charla into her car. She was leaving already. Shelby's hopes of speaking with her took a nosedive.

She shifted her gaze back to Ava. "I hate to ask for another favor, but is there any way you could persuade your mother to see me?"

Ava glanced toward her mother's car. "Things have been strained between us since Max and I became engaged, but I'll speak to her about it. I'd like to see the library establish my brother's memorial."

Sam said, "Shelby, Jocelyn tells me you believe something happened between Dylan and Leah at a Christmas party four years ago?"

Ava turned her startled gaze on Shelby. "What's he talking about?"

Unnerved by Sam's directness, Shelby crossed her arms and looked down. Anything she said with Ava present would surely get back to Charla. Shelby didn't want to lose what little chance she had of gaining Charla's support by gossiping about her son.

Without looking up, Shelby said, "It's nothing. Leah and I attended an office party together. She quit her job the next day."

"To marry Earl, right?" Ava asked.

Shelby shrugged. "I don't know what her reason was."

"But you think it had something to do with Dylan?" Sam's pointed question made Shelby realize why he was so successful as an FBI agent.

"As I said, I don't know what her reason was."

From the corner of her eye she saw Clint walking toward them. Sarah, too cute in a frilly pink dress and straw bonnet with a pink bow, skipped along at his side.

When Sarah caught sight of Shelby, she dropped her uncle's hand and raced to her friend. Happy for the interruption, Shelby crouched to catch the child in a hug. "Oh, Sarah, I've missed you."

Grinning, Sarah patted her own head. "Look, I got a hat."

"It's beautiful."

Nodding, the little girl said solemnly, "I know."

The adults around her chuckled.

Clint, catching Sarah's hand again, looked at Sam. "Are there any new leads?"

They all knew he was talking about his sister.

Sam shook his head. "We're still actively working the case. We haven't stopped looking."

Clint pressed a hand to his eyes and nodded. "I understand. All through the service I was praying something would surface today. It's Easter. She should be here with us."

Shelby threw her arms around him. "We're all praying for her, Clint."

"Thanks." He drew back to look at her. "Any more threats?"

Sam's brows snapped into a fierce frown. "Threats? Why haven't I heard about this?"

Shelby tried to make light of the situation. She didn't want Clint or her friends to worry about her.

"It's nothing concrete. The sheriff's office isn't even sure the incidents are related. Someone left a note on my car last week. Then Thursday someone left a message in lipstick on the mirror at the library."

"Don't forget the snake in the return book bin," Clint added.

Shelby managed a smile. How could she ever forget that? "Sheriff Reed thinks it was an April Fool's joke by some of the high school boys."

Sam said, "I don't take any kind of threat lightly. Any idea who's behind them?"

Shelby crossed her arms as a sudden chill ran down her spine. "No. They're so vague. 'Keep my mouth shut.' 'Don't talk about what I saw.' I have no idea what it is that I'm supposed to have seen. I'm hoping it's someone's idea of a joke."

She looked around. Was she being watched now? Was that someone here at church, blending into the crowd of worshipers while harboring evil in his or her heart?

"When did these threats start?" Sam demanded.

"The last day of March."

A speculative look crossed Sam's face as he stared at Patrick. "The day after Rivers arrived in town."

"Yes." Shelby glanced at Coral and Wendell, standing with a group of Wendell's supporters. How far would someone in Loomis go to keep secrets?

Patrick was encouraged by Max's assertion that his office could locate the missing deed. Looking over Max's shoulder, Patrick saw Mrs. Pershing approaching.

She stopped at Max's side and took his arm. "May I talk to you privately, son?"

Sending an apologetic look in Patrick's direction, Max said, "Of course. If you'll excuse us?"

"Sure."

"What now, Mother?" Max's tone was definitely cool as he took his mother's elbow to lead her away.

"I want you to come to Easter dinner at my place. It'll be just like old times."

As the Pershings walked away, Shelby left her friends and came to stand beside Patrick. "How's everything?"

"No one is pointing and yelling 'rapist' at the top of their lungs. But I can see I'll never be truly accepted in Loomis. Max thinks he can get to the bottom of the missing deed this week."

She bit her bottom lip. "Does that mean you'll be leaving soon?"

He should, but he didn't want to leave. Not yet. The pull of Shelby's clear gaze was keeping him here—for now. Soon he'd have to leave, but today was a day for the two of them.

"Are you trying to get rid of me?"

"Of course not."

Sarah ran over to tug on Shelby's hand. "Come play with me."

Sarah pointed to the playground equipment at the day care center, her almond-shaped bright green eyes alight with eagerness. "Swing me."

Shelby looked at Clint and he nodded. She beamed at the child. "Let's go."

Patrick walked beside them as they crossed to the playground. At the church steps, he saw Wyatt and his wife standing with his sons. Barb, camera in hand, was trying to get the boys to stand still for a picture in their Easter suits in front of the church doors.

Patrick was surprised when Wyatt nodded in his direction. Smiling, he nodded in return and took hold of Shelby's hand. It was turning out to be a pretty good day.

Sarah ran to one of the swings and climbed aboard. "Push me, Shelby."

"All right. Hold on tight. Wait a minute." Shelby slipped the elastic band from beneath the little girl's chin and removed her hat, Looking around, Shelby's eyes settled on Patrick. Holding out the straw bonnet, she said, "Here. Make yourself useful."

"Yes, ma'am." He took the hat and settled himself on a nearby bench.

Grasping the chains, Shelby took a few steps back and let go. Sarah giggled as she swung forward.

"Higher!"

"Okay." Shelby gave a hearty shove and Sarah sailed up into the air with a squeal, kicking her legs in delight.

Shelby was so good with the child. Patrick couldn't get over how natural she looked swinging her friend's daughter. She should have kids of her own.

What was the matter with the men in Loomis that they ignored a jewel like Shelby in their midst?

Wyatt's young son came running up to take the swing next to Sarah. He only had time to lie across the seat and push himself back and forth twice before his mother called out, "Mark Gerard, don't you dare get your suit dirty. Hurry up and c'mon, or we're leaving without you."

The empty threat made the boy smile, but he left the swing. Hurrying back the way he'd come, he plowed to a stop beside Patrick. "We're going to the cabin for a *whole week* and I'm gonna catch me a fish *twice* as big as the last one."

"Sounds like fun."

"Mark, am I gonna have to send your daddy to get you?" Barb was already at the car.

"No, ma'am," the boy yelled, and took off.

As Mark left, Clint came to join Patrick, followed by Ava and Max.

"Higher, Shelby!" Sarah yelled again.

Shelby laughed and shook her hands. "My arms are falling off."

"It's time to go, Sarah." Clint was obviously loath to end her fun. Shelby slowed the swing to a stop.

"Don't want to," Sarah pouted.

"It's time to eat," Clint stated firmly.

Ava stepped toward the girl and bent to her level. "Max and I are coming to your house. Just the two of us."

She glanced over her shoulder at Max. He nodded as some message passed between them. So he'd declined his mother's invitation to dinner. Patrick couldn't blame him.

Ava turned back to Sarah. "We made a huge picnic basket

with all kinds of goodies for our lunch, and I think we're going to help you hunt for Easter eggs in your backyard."

"Yea!" Sarah jumped out of the swing and dashed to Ava. Looking at Patrick, Sarah held up her hand. "Hat, please."

He handed the straw bonnet to Ava and she adjusted it on Sarah's blond curls. With their faces so close together, Patrick couldn't help but notice how much the two of them looked alike.

As they all left, Shelby came and stood by his side. She said, "It's really nice of Max and Ava to include Clint and Sarah in their plans today."

"Did you ever notice how much they look alike?"

"Sarah and Clint?"

"No. Sarah and Ava. They both have the same eyes."

"I guess I never noticed." Shelby turned to him. "Are you up for an Easter egg hunt?"

"Me?"

She nodded. "Ava and Clint invited us to join them. I didn't want to answer for you."

He nodded. "I'd like that."

What he really liked was the way her face brightened into a wide beaming smile.

Soak it in, because you won't be seeing it for long.

Suddenly California had never seemed so far away or less inviting.

TWELVE

Driving back to his house that evening, Patrick was distracted from thoughts of Shelby by the vibration of his cell phone in his pocket. Fumbling for the phone, he pulled it out.

Flipping it open, he was surprised to hear Ray Bailey, a coworker from California saying, "Hey dude, how's it going?"

"Not bad, Ray."

"Glad to hear it. Are you, like, winding things up and heading back to L.A. soon?"

Although the head mechanic at Wolfwind Cycles was trying to sound nonchalant, Patrick wasn't fooled. Ray never engaged in chitchat.

"What's wrong?"

After blowing out a long breath, Ray said, "We need you back as soon as you can get here."

"What do you need me for that Carl can't handle with both hands tied behind his back?"

"Everything," Ray shot back. "Carl's in the hospital."

Patrick's brows snapped into a scowl. "What happened?"

"He cracked up his bike on the freeway. Some airhead with a cell phone pressed to her ear cut him off and sent him skidding off the road."

Carl Wolf was Patrick's mentor and his friend, a man who

believed in Patrick's talent when no one else did. "He's going to be okay? Right?"

"He's got a busted leg and a busted arm, plus he took a hard knock to the head, but Carl is a tough nut. Dude, this ain't his first wreck."

"What are the doctors telling you?"

"They say he's going to be okay, but for now they're keeping him on some pretty heavy pain meds. He sure won't be able to work for a few weeks. Pat, we need you here. You know more about running the business than all the rest of us combined."

Raking a hand through his hair, Patrick took a second to compose his thoughts and lay out a plan. "All right, here's what you do. Debby in the front office knows how to do the payroll, and she can take over the accounting. Make sure everyone gets paid. How many new bikes are on order?"

"I'm not sure. Just a second." Muted background voices told Patrick that Ray was conferring with others. A minute later Ray came back on the line. "We've got six in production and five new orders. Carl's waiting for you to get back and start the designs on those and review them with the customers."

"Call Frank Parks over at Sunset Cycles. He does good freelance work. See if he can take on some of the projects so we can get them in the pipeline."

He pictured Shelby standing across the church lawn and smiling at him earlier. He could leave without selling the house, and he wouldn't be any worse off than before he'd come.

Except for one thing. He didn't want to leave. Not yet.

"Ray, I'm not going to be able to get back for a few days. The wildcat has a leaking gasket."

"Bummer! Are you, like, totally stranded in the swamp?"

Patrick chuckled. "No, I can ride her as long as I keep adding oil, but I don't want to take her cross-country this way. I've got a new gasket ordered, but it's going to take a couple of days to get here. You're going to have to handle the shop until I get back."

"Dude, I don't know about that. Carl will have my head if I mess up."

His reluctance made Patrick grin as he stepped out of his rental car. "Then don't mess up."

"Okay, but get back here as soon as you can, Pat. We need you."

Snapping the phone shut, Patrick continued to stare at it. He should get back. He could catch a flight out of New Orleans and have the bike shipped. It would be the fastest way to get to L.A. and handle things. He was needed there, but he wanted so much to stay here with Shelby.

He stuffed the phone in his pocket. A couple of days wouldn't make a major difference to the business. He'd wait for the new gasket and ride back. He'd wait and spend a couple more days in Loomis. A couple more days with Shelby.

By Monday evening, Shelby was still walking on air. Easter Sunday spent with Patrick would go down as one of the best days of her life.

It was all she had talked about at the Café Au Lait that morning. She'd tolerated the teasing of Wendy and Jocelyn about falling for Patrick, but in truth, she *had* fallen for him. Hard.

To see him in church listening, really listening, to the sermon Reverend Harmon had preached. To see him helping Sarah find eggs and laughing at her antics later in the afternoon. It made Shelby smile just to think about it.

A sense of hope for his well-being spread through her, warming her like the flames of a fire.

Perhaps he could start to see the good in his life and not just the bitterness he'd lived with for so long. She tucked that hope deep inside her heart for safekeeping.

In the cheerful yellow kitchen of her own home, Shelby set the oven to preheat and then cracked two eggs into a large glass mixing bowl.

If only she could crack Charla Renault's defenses as easily. Her second attempt to gain an audience with the woman that afternoon had been as fruitless as the first one. Shelby could still hear Bosworth's stoical tone. "Mrs. Renault is unavailable."

Unavailable. Like the money to start Shelby's new project.

As she mixed the batter for the brownie treats she would serve tomorrow after Story Hour, Shelby considered how she could get her idea off the ground without the Renault money.

The board might support her plan, but the funding simply wouldn't be available without a large donation.

After spreading the batter in a glass cake pan, Shelby slipped the mix into the oven and set the timer. What she needed was a new plan, another potentially magnanimous benefactor.

Suddenly, thoughts of Leah intruded. Shelby pressed the back of her hand to her forehead.

What am I doing worrying about brownies and money for books when Leah is still missing and a murderer is still loose in our city? What's wrong with me?

The realization that she couldn't keep holding on to hope settled over her like a heavy blanket of depression.

Worry, prayers, sorrow, nothing made time stand still.

Children would come to Story Hour tomorrow. They would devour her treats, smiling and giggling with chocolate smeared on their faces. Leah might be dead, but life would go on.

Setting the bowl in the sink, Shelby filled it with water, then went to her living room and settled herself in the recliner.

From the small table beside her chair, she picked up the Bible that had belonged to her mother and her grandmother before her. Knowing the words would soothe her worries and her heart, she opened the book and thumbed through the pages until she came to Psalms 86. She began to read.

> Bow down thine ear, O LORD, hear me: for I am poor and needy.
> Preserve my soul; for I am holy: O thou my God, save thy servant that trusteth in thee.
> Be merciful unto me, O Lord: for I cry unto thee daily.
> Rejoice the soul of thy servant: for unto thee, O Lord, do I lift up my soul.
> For thou, Lord, art good, and ready to forgive; and plenteous in mercy unto all them that call upon thee.
> Give ear, O LORD, unto my prayer; and attend to the voice of my supplications.
> In the day of my trouble I will call upon thee: for thou wilt answer me.

Yes, the words she knew so well drew her in and gave her the comfort she needed tonight.

Forty minutes later, the sound of the oven timer going off made her lay her Bible on the side table and head into the kitchen.

Donning an oven mitt, she pulled out the pan. The tempting smell of her rich dark chocolate treat was almost enough to make her cut herself a piece, but she resisted. These were for the kids tomorrow.

After setting the pan to cool on a wire rack, she walked back into her living room.

Her Bible lay closed on the chair seat.

Hadn't she put it on the side table? Was she losing her mind? Shaking her head at her own absentmindedness, Shelby picked up the book and noticed a sprig of red hairs jutting from the top of the pages like a bookmark.

She would have remembered if she had closed the book on her hair and yanked out this much. She'd done it more than once at the library.

Using her thumbnail, she opened to the pages the red strands marked to see a message written in black marker.

Time to die, Shelzie.

THIRTEEN

Patrick glanced at the clock for the tenth time in the last hour. The hands were barely past nine-forty. It was Monday night and he'd gone a whole day without seeing Shelby.

He paced the confines of his house knowing he had no reason to see her except that he wanted to be near her.

And he'd be leaving soon. She should know that.

He glanced at the clock. It was too late for a casual visit. What reason could he give?

He shook his head. *This is just what she needs, a second stalker.*

What if something else had happened at the library today? Would she have let him know?

Pulling his cell phone from his pocket, he stared at it. He couldn't call and talk to her because he didn't know her number.

There's always the phone book.

What were the odds an attractive single woman had a listed number?

Not good. But what would it hurt to look?

After striding into the kitchen, he pulled open a drawer and lifted out a dog-eared copy of the Loomis listings.

He could call and say what? *Miss you? Wish you were here with me tonight? You brighten my life?*

He might be thinking those things but he wasn't ready to say them out loud.

This attraction he felt for Shelby had happened much too fast. He needed to slow down, take a step back. Get an idea for how she was feeling about the whole thing.

She invited you to church.

So? Shelby helped people. That's what she did. She felt sorry for him because she hadn't spoken up in his defense ten years ago, and she was trying to make up for it now.

He might believe that was all that was going on if he hadn't looked into her eyes.

One thing was certain. This short time with Shelby wasn't enough.

You know I haven't been one for praying the last few years, Lord. You and I sort of lost each other, but I'm sorry. I'm looking for a little help now. What do You want from me? Why bring me back here?

His stepfather was gone. Patrick couldn't repair that rift even if he wanted to. He and Wyatt were at least talking, but their old friendship would never be the same.

That left Shelby. Was she the reason he was here? Try as he might, Patrick couldn't see how they could have any kind of relationship unless she were willing to give up her life here and travel out to L.A.

Shelby in Los Angeles. Even the idea of it made him smile. Talk about unlikely. She loved her hometown.

He opened the phone book. It didn't take him long to locate her name and her number.

Silly woman, she had her phone number and address listed for everyone to see.

Not silly. Naive, trusting, a perfect victim for the evil that slipped through Loomis as silent as a hungry gator slipping through the murky waters of the swamps.

Okay, you've got her number. Just call her.

Patrick opened his cell phone and punched in her number. Raising it to his ear, he listened to a recorded message.

"We're sorry. The number you have dialed is currently out of order."

He scowled as he listened to the message repeat itself. He snapped his phone closed as an uneasy feeling settled in the pit of his stomach.

What was Wendy's last name? He couldn't remember. He settled for calling Clint Herald. His home number and the number of his construction company were easy to find.

Clint picked up on the second ring.

Feeling a bit foolish, Patrick explained why he was calling. "I'm trying to get a hold of Shelby, but her line is out of order. Do you have a cell phone number for her?"

"Of course. Let me get it."

Patrick scribbled the number in the margin of the phone book. "Thanks, Clint."

"No problem. Thanks for keeping an eye on Shelby. She's very dear to me."

Patrick swallowed hard. Clint was the kind of man Shelby needed. Someone with roots in the community she loved. She already adored Sarah. If Sarah's mother never came home, Shelby would make the perfect substitute.

Patrick shook the thought from his mind. Shelby and Clint were close friends—that was all.

"You say her phone is out of order? That's odd," Clint mused. "I spoke to her about half an hour ago. I know she's home. She called me and said she was baking brownies for the kids at the library tomorrow. She wanted to know if I could bring Sarah by."

"I'll try her cell phone."

"If she doesn't answer, can you go check on her, Patrick? Sarah is already in bed, or I'd go myself."

"No problem. I'm sure she's fine, but I'll have her call you just to set your mind at rest."

"Great."

Clint hung up and Patrick dialed Shelby's cell phone. It rang and rang then turned over to voice mail. He left a brief message.

Snapping his phone shut, he stared at it for a long minute. Spinning around, he snatched up his bike keys and headed outside.

Someone was in the house.

Horrified, Shelby dropped her Bible and spun around.

The heavy thud of her heart stopped her breath. Fear gagged her, draining the strength from her limbs.

Her gaze flew around the room, seeking the intruder.

Where was he? In the closet? In the bathroom? Upstairs? Behind her?

She whirled around, checking the long drapes at the window for the telltale bulge of someone hiding there.

They blew inward and flipped slightly in a gentle breeze. Shelby knew she hadn't opened the window.

Get out! Get out of here!

Her mind screamed the words, but she didn't make a sound. Couldn't move. The distant ringing of her cell phone made her head snap around. She barely heard it over the pounding of her pulse in her ears.

The phone was in her purse—out in the entryway on her grandmother's cherry sideboard.

Was it a trick to get her to rush out there? Uncertainty and terror kept her rooted to the spot. Then the ringing stopped.

Please, Lord—please Lord—give me strength. Help me think.

She needed a weapon. From the coffee table, she snatched up the cut glass candy dish Wendy had given her for Christmas. It wasn't much, but it helped to have something in her hands.

It took Herculean strength to move toward the kitchen. Her house phone hung on the wall just inside the doorway. If she could reach it, she could call 9-1-1.

Her gaze darted around the living room, checking every corner.

Where was he? What did he want?

A board creaked near the top of the stairs. The old house always creaked, but was that a footstep?

She managed a second step. A third agonizing movement brought her into contact with the wall. She pressed her back to it and relished the small sense of comfort. She worked her way to the kitchen door.

Taking her eyes off the living room to reach for the phone took more willpower than she knew she possessed.

Quickly, she grabbed the hard plastic receiver, punched in 9-1-1 with trembling fingers and held the phone to her ear.

Her eyes returned to scanning the room and the stairwell that led up to her bedroom. It took several seconds for Shelby to realize the phone in her hand was dead.

No dial tone. No police. No help.

"Why are you doing this?" She tried to shout the words, but they barely made it out of her dry mouth.

She bit her lower lip until she tasted blood. "This is a bad dream."

Only it wasn't. She was so scared. Her ragged breathing changed to broken sobs. "Please, God, make this not be happening."

Forcing herself to leave the relative safety of the wall, she flung herself across the kitchen. At the far counter, she dropped the candy dish to the floor and pulled a butcher knife from the rack. Whirling around, she held the knife in front of her with both hands.

The solid feel of the wooden handle gave her some much-needed strength. She checked the basement door to her left. The sliding bolt was still latched. No one had opened it.

She could get outside by going through the cellar, but there was no way she was going down those stairs.

Instead, she made her way back into the living room, keeping the wall at her back. Slide one step. Skirt the sofa. Get back to the wall.

Again, she heard creaking. Was it her rocker?

Shelby glanced from the stairs to the archway leading to her entryway. She could dart to the front door before anyone could get down the stairs.

If he was up there. If he was alone. If someone wasn't waiting for her around the corner in the entry or in the coat closet beside the front door.

The sound of an engine outside made her think of Patrick. Would she ever see him again?

If she died tonight, he'd never know how much she cared. *Don't think like that.*

She'd reached the opening to the entryway. It was now or never.

Spinning around, she faced the open archway with her knife held out ready to stab anything that moved. Could she? Oh, yes!

Slipping into the foyer, she quickly turned left, then right, checking the room. It was bare. She whirled around to check behind her. The living room remained empty.

The doorbell shattered the silence. She spun to face the front door. Was someone toying with her? Did she dare open it?

"Who's there?" The words came out a harsh whisper. She swallowed hard.

Try again.

Loud pounding made her jump.

"Who's there?" Her voice squeaked, but it was audible.

"Shelby, it's Patrick."

Safety. The air whooshed out of her lungs. She rushed to the door and yanked it open.

FOURTEEN

Patrick staggered back a step as Shelby launched herself into his arms.

"Thank God you're here." She clung to his neck. Sobs racked her body.

"Honey, what's wrong?" He stoked her hair, trying to calm her.

Something clattered at his feet. Looking down, he saw she'd dropped a knife. A big knife.

Pushing free of his embrace, she frantically tugged on his hand. "Come on. We have to get out of here."

He followed her relentless pull out to the street. "Shelby, what's going on?"

"There's someone—in my house. I was so scared."

Fury roared through him. Whoever was doing this wouldn't get away this time. "Stay here."

She latched on to his arm with both hands. "No! Don't leave me."

Drawing her back into his embrace, he held her close. Torn between rushing off and consoling her, he chose the latter. "Okay, okay, you're safe with me now. Did you call the police?"

"I tried—the phone's dead."

He extracted his cell phone from his pocket, flipped it open and dialed 9-1-1 with one hand.

An operator came on the line immediately. "What is your emergency?"

"I want to report a break-in at 921 Merchant Street."

"Is the perpetrator still on the premises?"

"I don't know."

"Tell them to hurry," Shelby whispered against his chest.

Less than five minutes later there were two squad cars on the scene, their light bars flashing red and blue, illuminating the neighboring houses. Many of Shelby's neighbors came out to watch.

The deputies listened to Shelby's halting explanation of what had happened and then began a quick check of the house and the surrounding grounds.

Patrick waited beside Shelby, keeping one arm around her. It took less than ten minutes for the police to complete their sweep of the area.

Deputy Olson conferred with his partner on the front steps then came toward them. He tipped his head to one side as he studied Patrick. "Seems like you're always around when Miss Mason has a fright."

"Seems like you're never around when she does," Patrick replied, not liking the man's tone.

"Patrick, please." Shelby stepped in front of him and addressed Deputy Olson. "Did you find anything?"

"No, ma'am."

"We don't find any sign of a break-in." Deputy Bertrand added.

"He wrote in my Bible. He, or she, or they—used red hairs to mark the place. How is that not a sign of a break-in?"

The men exchanged pointed looks. "You say the perpetrator left red hairs in your Bible?" Olson's eyes narrowed as he peered at Shelby.

Twisting her hands together nervously, she said, "Yes. He used the strands like a bookmark."

"Where is this Bible?" Deputy Olson asked.

"On the floor by my recliner where I dropped it."

Again the men exchanged looks. Bertrand nodded. "I'll check it out. Miss Mason, y'all come with me to see if anything is missing."

Shelby started forward, followed closely by Patrick.

Deputy Olson stopped Patrick by putting one hand on his chest. "I'm afraid you're gonna have to wait here. I'll take your statement while Miss Mason has a look around."

One of Shelby's neighbors, a woman in her midsixties, came across the street holding her pink bathrobe closed with one hand. "Land sakes, child. What's going on?"

Shelby managed a slight smile. "Someone broke in, Mrs. Kelly."

"Are you all right?"

"I'm fine. Just frightened."

Deputy Olson tipped his hat. "Ma'am, I'm going to have to ask y'all to step back until we're finished processing the scene."

She pressed her hands to her cheeks. "My goodness gracious, this is just like an episode from that crime show on TV."

As Mrs. Kelly retreated to share what she knew with other neighbors, Shelby wished it were a television show and not her life exposed for everyone to see. She'd be the topic of speculation in every hair salon and grocery store in Loomis before noon tomorrow.

Even with the officer at her side, Shelby had a hard time reentering her own house.

The entryway looked the same as always. The dark hardwood floor gleamed in the light from the wall sconce. The dried flower arrangement was reflected in the mirror over the antique sideboard. Her purse was still lying there. Nothing had changed.

She shivered. Only nothing was really the same.

Deputy Aaron Bertrand stood beside her coat closet holding a plastic bag that contained her butcher knife.

Clasping her arms across her middle, she decided she was definitely getting that can of mace Wendy had been harping about.

The deputy nodded at her. "Can y'all tell if anything is missing, Miss Mason?"

She checked the contents of her purse. "Everything seems to be here."

"How about the rest of the house?"

"I really don't have anything of value. Some family jewelry, but it's not expensive. I don't keep cash on hand."

"Take a look around. If you find something is missing later, you can always file a report then. I know this is hard. There's no one else in the house. I checked." His tone brimmed with understanding.

She walked into the living room. The phone lay on the floor where she had dropped it just inside the kitchen. She could hear the faint sound of an automated voice saying, "If you'd like to make a call, please hang up and try again."

Baffled, Shelby looked at the officer beside her. "The phone was dead when I tried to call 911."

He picked it up. "It seems to be working now."

"I'm telling you, it was dead." She hadn't imagined it.

"Yes, ma'am."

Glancing around the room, Shelby couldn't see anything out of place. The deputy walked ahead of her up the stairs. She hesitated at the first tread.

This is my home. I will not be afraid in my own home.

Only she was. Very afraid. Someone had come in, watched

her, written their evil words in her family Bible. How could such a devious person live among them without being detected?

She had no answers. Only faith that goodness would triumph in the end.

Forcing herself forward, she climbed the steps.

In her bedroom everything seemed in place. She opened the wooden jewelry box on her dresser. Her small diamond earrings were still there, along with her mother's antique pearl brooch. Nothing had been disturbed.

She should be grateful that she hadn't been robbed, but she wasn't. Robbery she could understand.

Time to die, Shelzie.

Who wanted her dead? Why? None of it made sense.

And that made it so much more frightening.

Shelby walked through all the rooms in the house looking for anything out of place, but found nothing unusual. When they reached the living room again, she turned to Deputy Bertrand. Nothing seems to be missing."

"That's a blessing, ma'am."

It was. *She* could be missing—like Leah.

Had her friend known the same kind of mind-numbing terror as someone stalked her? Shelby prayed she hadn't.

She pressed a hand to her forehead. "I'd like my Bible back as soon as you're done with it."

"We didn't find a Bible, Miss Mason."

She spun around to stare at her chair. "I dropped it right there. Maybe it fell under the chair."

Shelby sank to her knees and checked under all the furniture. Sitting back on her heels, she looked at him. "It's gone."

"All this fella took was a Bible?"

"Yes."

"Odd thing for a thief to take, isn't it?" The suspicion in his tone shocked her.

"You don't believe me?" She scrambled to her feet.

"I'm not saying that. I'm just saying it's an odd thing for a thief to take. You say there were red hairs in the book."

"Yes."

"Could it have been your own hair?"

She considered the possibility. "No. It was darker and short—only a few inches long."

His eyes narrowed. "Are you sure?"

Shelby sucked in a sharp breath. "Red hair was found at the murder scenes of both Earl and Dylan. Do you think their murderer was here?"

"I'm afraid I can't comment on that, Miss Mason." He closed his notebook. "We're still waiting to hear if your lipstick was a match to that on the mirror."

"I didn't write that note."

"But you can't produce the note you say you found on your car or this Bible?"

"Are you suggesting I'm making this all up?"

"Stranger things have happened. We'll have our patrol cars come by frequently tonight. You'll be fine if you keep all your doors and windows locked." He turned and walked out.

Alone, Shelby clasped her arms across her chest and fought back a shiver as she glanced around the room. Would her stalker be back?

A sound made her whirl to face the entryway. Patrick stood watching her, his eyes filled with concern. He crossed the room and took her hand. She gripped it tight.

He jerked his head toward the door. "Come on."

She followed him until they reached the sidewalk, where his pace quickened. She hurried to keep up with him. She had to. He had a death grip on her hand.

Death grip. Poor choice of words.

"Patrick, where are you taking me?"

"Somewhere safe. You're not staying here alone. I'd offer to stay here with you, but I'm sure you'd object to that."

She looked back at her house. "At this point, not as loudly as you might think."

When they reached his bike parked across the street, Shelby slipped on behind him and wrapped her arms around his waist. "I thought your bike was broken."

"It's leaking a little oil, but it'll run." He patted her hands. Shelby loosened her grip. "Too tight?"

"No, you can hold on tighter if you need to."

She took him up on his offer. "Where are we going?"

"Somewhere this nutcase won't expect you to go."

"L.A., Paris, Cincinnati?"

The roar of the engine drowned out his chuckle and soon they were cruising through the streets of town.

He made sharp turns and took occasional shortcuts through alleys. Shelby realized he was trying to make sure they weren't being followed. She checked behind them frequently but never saw anyone.

When they reached the edge of town, he sped up and the night blew past as they flew down the highway. If only the rush of wind could blow her fear away as well.

Several miles from town, Patrick slowed and turned onto a rutted dirt track that led back into the bayou.

The rough road made slow going on the bike. Trees pressed in close. Spanish moss from the limbs overhead brushed against her in the darkness like ghostly fingers. The damp air held the smell of rotting vegetation underlying the pungent scent of the woods.

Once, something flapped past them. A heron, perhaps, disturbed by their passing. The bumpy road finally ended, and Shelby looked over Patrick's shoulder to see a small cabin tucked back into the trees. Light poured out the windows, proving someone was home.

He killed the bike engine, and the chirpings, croaking sounds of the swamp took over the night.

Resting her cheek against Patrick's back again, she didn't get off, but stayed put with her arms around him.

He was so warm and strong.

He covered her hands with one of his own. They sat in the dark without speaking, without moving. Simply drawing strength from their contact.

The front porch light snapped on and a man's voice called out, "Who's there?"

FIFTEEN

Taking Shelby's hand, Patrick led her up to the porch. The look of surprise on Wyatt's face in the yellow light from a single bulb over the doorway would have been comical if things weren't so serious.

"Wyatt, I need a favor." Patrick drew Shelby in front of him and placed his hands on her shoulders. "Shelby needs someplace safe to stay tonight."

Patrick heard Wyatt's wife call out from inside the house. "Honey, who is it?"

A second later, she appeared at his elbow drying her hands on a white dish towel. Dressed in jeans and an oversized shirt that looked like it might belong to her husband, Barb's cheerful round face registered curiosity, surprise and then recognition in quick succession. "Shelby Mason, what are y'all doing here?"

Shelby twisted her head to look up at him. "Patrick, I don't think this is a good idea."

"What's going on?" Wyatt demanded without moving out of the doorway.

Patrick met his gaze. "Shelby is in trouble. Someone has been making threats against her. They broke into her home tonight."

"And you brought her here?" Wyatt's brows snapped into a frown of displeasure.

"You poor thing." Barb pulled her husband's arm off the doorjamb and started to open the screen door. "Y'all come right in. How horrible. I don't know what this town is coming to when a body isn't safe in their own home."

"Barb, this is none of our business," Wyatt said as he gripped her shoulder.

Patrick sighed. "I didn't know where else to go. I don't know who we can trust."

An odd expression flitted across Wyatt's face. "Why trust me?"

"You were my best friend, Wyatt. I'd trust you with my life, and with hers."

Barb laid her hand on her husband's arm. "Let Shelby stay here. It's the Christian thing to do."

Wyatt pressed his lips into a thin line, and then nodded.

Relief unlocked Patrick's tense muscles. He gave Shelby a gentle nudge, and she reluctantly stepped into the house. Patrick followed her. After scanning the road behind them, he closed the door and faced Wyatt.

His friend was watching his wife hustle Shelby into the kitchen with the promise of a strong cup of coffee. He met Patrick's gaze. "Is this related to the murders? Have you called the cops?"

"The police checked out Shelby's place but didn't find anything. I can't say I have much faith in Bradford Reed's force."

"No, the old guy is working harder at hanging on until he can collect a full pension than he is at solving local crimes."

"Whoever did this is smart enough to cover their tracks."

Barb walked back into the room and propped her hands on her hips. "You're not leaving us out of this discussion. Y'all get your buns into this kitchen so we can hear what's going on. This is no time to be leaving the womenfolk in the dark."

Patrick and Wyatt exchanged amused looks. Wyatt motioned Patrick toward the door to the other room. "Better do as she says or she'll take her granny's cast iron skillet to the side of your head."

Barb rolled her eyes and returned to the other room.

Settling around the oval, red Formica table in the kitchen, Patrick waited until Barb had finished serving coffee and taken a seat. In the bright, cheery setting, he was glad to see the fearful, haunted look retreating from Shelby's eyes.

"What kind of threats have you been getting?" Wyatt asked.

"A note on her car to keep her mouth shut. A cottonmouth snake in the return book bin at the library."

"Wait a minute." Barb held up a hand. "The kids and I were there that day. I thought the police said it was just a prank."

Shaking his head, Patrick said, "Too coincidental. It happened the day after the first note. Someone wanted Shelby to know they could make good on their threat."

Shelby took a sip of her coffee and set the blue earthenware mug onto the matching saucer. "After that, there was a note in lipstick on the mirror at the library. Then tonight." She shivered, and Patrick longed to take her in his arms.

"Someone broke into her house."

Throwing out one hand for emphasis, Shelby said, "I walked from my chair to the kitchen and took a pan of brownies out of the oven. By the time I walked back into my living room he had written 'Time to die, Shelzie' in my Bible."

Barb pressed a hand to her lips. "You poor child."

Shelby swept her hair back from her face. "I still don't know how the phone could be dead one minute and then working when the police came without any sign of tampering to the lines."

"Oh, that's easy," Barb said. "My son once put a toy flag in the phone jack in our spare bedroom. Our phone was out of service for two days before a repairman found it."

"What night do you think he's talking about?" Wyatt stared into his cup.

Patrick reached over to take Shelby's hand. "This all started when I came back to town. I think this is about the night Coral said I assaulted her."

"What could Shelby know about that night?" Wyatt still didn't look up. There was an odd tone in his voice that made Patrick study him closely.

"I overheard Coral tell someone she intended to sleep with Patrick."

Wyatt's gaze shot up. "Who?"

"I didn't see who it was." Shelby's voice revealed how tired she was, how much her fright had taken out of her.

Wyatt relaxed a fraction and Patrick's curiosity rose.

"Maybe we're wrong about this," Shelby continued. "Maybe it has to do with the night Earl was killed or the night Leah disappeared. I don't know. My brain is fried from trying to make sense of it."

Barb rose to her feet. "The cure for fried brain is a good night's sleep. Shelby, you can have one of the beds in the spare room. Mr. Rivers, I'm afraid it's a lumpy couch for you."

Shelby looked at Patrick. He winked at her. "Try and get some rest. Wyatt and I'll keep watch. If it makes you feel better, I'm sure Barb will let you put her skillet under your pillow."

He was rewarded with a small but genuine smile that lifted his heart.

As she followed Barb out of the room, Patrick's hands clenched into fists.

Wyatt rose and took his coffee mug to the sink. "What's the plan?"

"For tonight, keep a sharp eye out for anything suspicious."

"And after tonight?"

"I'm not sure."

"You like her a lot, don't you?"

Patrick rolled his mug between his palms. "Yeah. She's one special lady."

"I never figured you'd fall for a quiet one."

"Me, neither. I used to go for the flashy ones, not the brainy ones."

"Like Coral?"

Patrick hesitated. He wasn't sure he wanted to dig into the past, but he wanted Wyatt to understand. To forgive him.

"About that, Wyatt. I honestly didn't know you were in love with her. I never would have taken her home if I had."

"Yeah, right." Bitterness colored his words. "Everything was going your way. A scholarship, captain of a championship team, pro scouts looking at you, girls falling all over you. Why did you have to have her, too?"

"I'm sorry. I don't know what else to say."

"My wife is a good Christian woman and she likes Shelby. That's the reason I'm letting you stay."

Wyatt jerked his head toward the door. "There's a shed out back. You can put your bike in there."

Someone was pointing down at her. Jeering at her. The floor was cold beneath her back. Her stomach hurt. She was going to be sick.

A man leaned toward her, his face swimming in and out of focus. It was Dylan. "Leah's watchdog is down for the count at last."

Shelby jolted awake, gasping for air. Her heart hammered in her chest.

Was someone there?

She peered into the gloom, trying to get her bearings, not daring to move.

Moonlight streamed though an unfamiliar window. A tall chest of drawers stood nearby. An oval mirror on the wall reflected the moonbeams across the bare wooden walls. This wasn't her room.

Little by little, the events of the past evening came back. She was at Wyatt's cabin. Patrick had brought her here to keep her safe.

Her nightmare faded as it always did. The recurring dream hadn't bothered her in months, but this time was different. This time the man's face belonged to Dylan Renault.

Slipping out of bed, she crossed to the door and eased it open.

"Shelby, is that you?"

His voice, so welcome and familiar, allowed her to draw a full breath brimming with relief. "Yes."

Patrick sat up on the sofa beneath a wide window. "What's the matter?"

"Bad dream."

He rubbed a hand over his face. "Want to talk about it?"

Crossing the room, she settled in a chair beside the sofa. "No. It's gone now. Where's Wyatt?"

"Keeping watch on the front porch." Patrick raised his wrist and tipped his watch face toward the window. "I'll go relieve him in a few minutes."

"I feel terrible about this." She drew her knees up and wrapped her arms around her legs.

"About what?"

"Keeping you up. Making Wyatt surrender his home. Everything."

"None of this is your fault."

"I know." Even to her own ears her voice sounded tiny and forlorn. Why did it feel as if she were to blame? She settled her chin on her knees.

Patrick patted the cushion beside him. "Come here."

She hesitated a fraction of a second, then bolted to his side. Wrapping his arms around her, he settled his chin on the top of her head as she burrowed against his shoulder. The steady beat of his heart beneath her ear brought her a deep feeling of security and a new ache deep in her chest.

He's only holding me because I'm frightened. He'd do the same for anyone. Even if I wish the reason was different, that he was holding me because he cares for me, I can't read more into this. He's being a friend.

It might be sensible advice, but it didn't help. She'd fallen for Patrick in a big way. Even the knowledge that heartbreak loomed on her horizon couldn't change the way she felt. He would be leaving soon and she would be staying.

What if he asks me to go to California?

How could she even think of leaving? Leah was still missing, Clint and Sarah needed her, Wendy and Jocelyn had already lost one dear friend—if she left they'd be losing another. No, her life was tied to Loomis by bonds too strong to be easily broken. She would stay, and she would miss him for the rest of her life, but at least she would have this time in his arms to remember.

He rubbed her shoulder. "Repeat after me. None of this is Shelby's fault."

"I should be braver."

"You want to be a woman who totes a gun and can shoot a cigarette out of a guy's mouth at twenty paces?"

She nodded vigorously. "Yes, I should be one of those women. Tough like Wendy."

"I kinda like your soft side."

She tilted her head to peer up at him. "You do?"

"You have no idea," he said softly.

The rapid thudding of her heart had nothing to do with fear and everything to do with the feel of his arms around her. The air suddenly shimmered with tension.

Slowly, he drew away. Leaning back, he blew out a deep breath. "You make it hard to keep my mind on business."

"I do?" She sat up, missing the warmth of his arms with an intensity that frightened her.

"I never thought I'd say this, but L.A. is going to seem tame after Loomis."

"Do you have to go back?" The foolish question was out of her mouth before she could stop it. She couldn't read his expression in the darkness. More than anything, she wanted to see his reaction.

"Everything I've worked so hard for is there." His voice held a wistful quality she didn't understand, but his words were answer enough.

Folding her arms tightly across her chest, she tried for a bright tone. "Of course you have to go back. Your life is there just like my life is here. We might have come from the same place, but we live in two separate worlds."

"I've been asking myself why God brought me back here. I sure never intended to see Loomis again."

"So, why *did* you come back?" It was easier to ask about his past than to think about a future without him.

"My stepfather left a rather odd will. If I came back to Loomis and personally went through the house, through all his things, I could sell the place and keep the money. If I didn't come, I got nothing."

"He must have wanted you to come back. Maybe he wanted you to have your mother's books."

"Then why not send them to me?"

She laid a hand on his arm. "Because then you wouldn't have had to face up to your past."

"Maybe."

Pulling her hand away, she asked, "What about your real father. Who was he?"

"I don't know much about him except that he was a fisherman. My mother told me he drowned when his boat sank in a storm. They'd only been married a few weeks."

"How terrible."

"She married Ben about six months later. Of course she was already pregnant with me. He never let me forget that I wasn't his son. But I wanted to be."

The longing in those words told her exactly how hard it had been for him growing up.

"I wanted him to be proud of me and come to my ballgames. I wanted him to tell his buddies what a great kid he had. But he never did."

"It was his loss. You can't blame yourself for that."

Patrick pushed himself to his feet. "Are you feeling better?"

"Yes, I am. Thank you." It wasn't exactly a lie. The terror of her nightmare had faded, although the need to bury her face in her pillow and weep away her sorrow had replaced it.

Patrick said, "I should go relieve Wyatt."

"Thanks for sitting with me," she managed to say past the lump in her throat.

"You should get some more sleep. I know it's hard, but try not to worry, Shelby. I won't let anyone hurt you."

It was too late, she thought as she watched him walk out into the night. He had already broken her heart.

SIXTEEN

Bright and early the next morning, Shelby sat on Wyatt's sofa and used her cell phone to call Wendy. It took fifteen minutes to fill her cousin in on the details.

"I'm fine, Wendy, but I'm not coming in to work for a few days."

"Where are you? I'm bringing you my .357."

"I don't need it. I have Patrick and Wyatt Tibbs to protect me. I'm safe here."

"All right. Don't worry about anything here. I've got it covered."

"I knew you would."

After the call to her cousin, Shelby phoned the police station and spoke to the officer in charge of her investigation. She wasn't surprised to find there was nothing new in the case. At least, nothing they were willing to share with her.

When she closed her cell phone, she looked up to see Patrick smiling at her from the doorway of the kitchen. He held out a mug. "I made coffee. Want some?"

"Always." She tucked her feet beneath her as she curled up on the end of the sofa.

"Any news?"

"I don't know why I thought they would have something

yet. It's going to take a while to process any prints they lifted. I've learned that much about police procedure from Jocelyn in the past few months. I'm not sure how hard they'll look for my missing Bible when they have a string of homicides still unsolved."

He strolled over and handed her the coffee.

"Where is everyone?"

"The kids are fishing with Wyatt, and Barb is photographing birds."

"I'm not going in to work today, but I can't hide out here forever, Patrick. What am I going to do?"

He ran his knuckles down her cheek. "Give the police a little more time to find out who's behind it."

"How much time?"

"I don't have the answers, Shelby. I wish I did."

Turning away from his touch, she said, "I'm giving this over to God. He is my rock and my salvation. I'll put my trust in Him."

"Amen," Barb said, coming through the door. "My, that coffee smells good. Are my men back?"

"Not yet." Patrick stepped away from Shelby.

She took a quick sip of her coffee to hide the blush she knew was staining her cheeks.

A few seconds later, the laughter of the boys and the thud of their small feet on the porch announced their arrival.

"Mom! Mom! You gotta see this. There's the coolest motorcycle in the whole world in our shed. Is that guy here?"

The boys practically fell over themselves getting into the room, but they stopped dead in their tracks at the sight of Shelby and Patrick.

Catching Patrick's eye, Shelby wrinkled her nose at him. "You've got another fan, Mr. Award Winner."

Patrick set his cup down and planted his hands on his hips. "So you like my bike, do you?"

Both of them nodded.

"Come on, I'll give you a close-up look."

"Cool. Can we take her for a spin?" Mark's eyes brightened.

Patrick shook his head. "I'm afraid not. I'm having some engine trouble, but you can sit on it."

"Awesome." They both turned and hurried out the door.

Barb picked up the camera she'd been using. "I have to get a picture of this. It is safe for them to be on it, isn't it? I mean—they can't start it or anything."

"I've got the key."

"Oh, good. Well, don't just stand around in here. It's a beautiful day. Come outside and let me get a picture of the two of you together. Come on, come on." She flapped her hand at them.

Chuckling, Shelby allowed Patrick to pull her to her feet and they followed Barb outside.

At the shed, Barb paused to study her shot, turning her head first one way, then the other. "The morning light coming in, contrasting with the sharp shadows, makes a good composition." She dropped to one knee. "Okay, Wyatt Jr., hop on."

Patrick grabbed the boy before he could scramble aboard. "Careful, there's a puddle of oil under it. I don't want you getting any on your shoes or your mom will skin me alive."

"I would, too." Barb grinned as she began snapping pictures with her digital camera.

"Is it broke?" Mark, squatting down beside Patrick's boots, put a finger in the oily dirt. He wrinkled his nose and his mother snapped another picture.

"No," Patrick said, "I just have to keep putting oil in it until I get a new gasket. The one I ordered should be at my house by now."

"What will you do then?"

Patrick's eyes met Shelby's. "Then I have to get back to L.A."

After Patrick lifted the boys off, Barb said, "Now you and Shelby get on. I want a few shots of y'all."

Holding up one hand, Shelby shook her head. "No. I look terrible. I slept in these clothes."

"Honey, you look fine."

Patrick leaned close to Shelby. His warm breath tickled her ear. "She's right, you look beautiful. Except you have a stray hair here." He brushed a hand over her head.

"And here." He tucked a strand behind her ear, letting his fingers linger there and sending shivers down her spine.

Batting his hand away, she muttered, "I'm good."

"Good enough."

Grasping the handlebars he swung his leg over the bike, then offered her a hand. She climbed on behind him and tried to smile at Barb.

These pictures might be all she had to remember him by.

"Put your arms around him, Shelby," Barb called out as she focused through her lens.

Shelby did, holding tight and wishing she could ride away with him.

Why not? What was stopping her?

Everything.

Shelby couldn't leave. Would Patrick even consider staying?

She glanced over to where Wyatt, quiet and withdrawn, watched them from the shadows at the side of the house.

Asking Patrick to subject himself to a life of constant mistrust was something she couldn't bring herself to do.

She would have to let him go and pray he found happiness elsewhere.

* * *

The rest of the day Patrick couldn't help noticing as Shelby became more and more distant. His teasing couldn't bring a smile to her face. After lunch, she spent a long time shut in her room.

He wasn't sure what was going on in her head. Was it worry over her stalker or something else?

After supper, he was finally able to catch up with her as she was sitting alone on the dock staring out into the bayou. She was throwing sticks into the water and watching the ripples spreading out.

Patrick walked up to stand behind her. "You need to be careful of gators out here all by yourself."

"Do they write death threats in Bibles and wear apricot glaze lipstick?" She threw another stick in with a vengeance.

"I've never seen one wearing anything but chartreuse." He folded his long legs pretzel style to sit beside her.

Breaking a twig in half, she tossed another small piece off the end of the dock. "Leah is out there somewhere."

"Shelby, you don't know that."

"You're right, I don't, but nothing else could keep her away from Sarah for so long. Why is God letting this happen?"

"Good question."

"One with no answers. How soon will you be leaving Loomis?"

"Is that what this is about?"

Will she miss me? Do I dare hope she feels the same way I do? She hung her head, and he couldn't see her face for the curtain of long red hair hiding it. Reaching out, he drew her tresses aside. "Come with me." He waited without breathing, praying she would say yes.

She didn't even look at him. "I can't." He couldn't believe how much her words hurt.

She scooted around to face him. "You could start your own motorcycle place. Not in Loomis, it's too small, but New Orleans is less than an hour away. There are lots of bike riders in the Big Easy."

"I have people depending on me in California. My boss had a bad wreck. The guys in the shop are holding it together, but they need someone in charge until Carl gets back on his feet."

A low rumble of thunder announced the approach of a storm over the bayou. The wind kicked up stirring the water and tugging at her hair.

She dropped her gaze and started breaking her last stick into tiny pieces. "I'm sorry. Of course you can't leave your friends in a lurch."

"My dream for the past nine years has been to become part owner of Wolfwind Cycles. This is my chance to prove to Carl that I'll make a good partner."

She nodded. "You have to follow your dream. I understand that."

His dreams had changed since meeting her again, but what good would it do to pine for something he couldn't have?

She sighed. "I'll miss you. You've been a good friend. Who's going to save me next time someone breaks into my place?"

"Where's your faith? Where is the woman who was turning her life over to God?"

She sniffed and wiped at her nose. "A gator got her."

Patrick couldn't stop himself. He drew her closer. "I'm not leaving until I'm sure you're safe."

It was a promise he intended to keep.

The storm rolled in a little after dark, trapping everyone inside the cabin.

Shelby sat near the window and watched with unease. She hated storms.

Lightning flashed as the wind lashed the trees and made the small cabin creak. The rain fell in sheets when it came, flooding the ruts of the road leading away from the property.

Barb sent the boys to bed early and came to sit beside Shelby. Patrick and Wyatt had taken up positions on the front porch.

Patting Shelby's arm, Barb said, "Don't worry. We wouldn't be trapped here. If the four-wheel drive on the truck can't get us out, we have a boat."

"It would be a bad night to be out on the water." Shelby winced as another bolt of lightning split the sky, followed by a crack of thunder.

"It would be a bad night to be out anywhere. Which is a good thing for you. No one's going to find you in this storm."

"You're probably right about that."

"I'm going to bed, dear. I suggest y'all do the same. The men are taking turns keeping watch, just like last night. You'll be safe."

Safe from her stalker but not from a broken heart.

Shelby retired to her room, but she couldn't fall asleep. She lay in bed listening to the sound of the rain on the roof. Gradually, the thunder grew fainter as the storm moved away.

She must have fallen asleep, because she woke with a start a few hours later. She sat up listening for what had disturbed her. Then she heard it. The sound of an engine coming closer. It didn't sound like a car.

Abruptly, the engine cut off.

She waited, but it never started again. Had it been a boat? Had her stalker found her hiding place?

Throwing back the cotton coverlet, she climbed out of bed and walked into the living room. "Patrick?"

There was no answer.

Crossing her arms over her chest, she moved to stare out

the window. A bright three-quarter moon hung low in the sky, casting long shadows among the trees outside. Overhead, a few lingering clouds drifted. A smattering of raindrops fell again. The breeze picked up, making the shadows move.

Was that a man in the trees?

She strained her eyes to see better. Was someone watching the cabin?

She took a quick step back from the window and pressed a hand to her mouth.

The dark shape she watched took one more step into the clearing just as the moon came out from beneath the clouds. A marsh deer raised its head to sniff the night air, and Shelby nearly collapsed with relief.

A nervous giggle escaped her lips.

She was expecting the boogeyman and got Bambi instead.

Thank goodness she hadn't roused the house.

Taking a moment to catch her breath, Shelby admired the sleek form of the animal outside. Suddenly, the deer leaped away, its white tail raised in alarm a second before it disappeared from sight.

The shadow of a man crossed in front of the window and the door opened. Shelby froze.

He must have heard her quick, indrawn breath because he looked toward her. "Shelby?"

"Patrick. Oh, thank goodness." She raced to him, but he held her off.

"I'll get you wet."

She stepped back. "What were you doing out in the rain?"

"I thought I heard something." He shrugged out of his borrowed rain jacket.

"The engine?"

He paused in the act of hanging up his coat to stare at her. "You heard it, too?"

"Yes. Did you find out what it was?"

"No, but it could have been a boat. Gator hunters often prowl the bayou at night. Everything looks fine outside. Go back to bed."

"All right." She reluctantly did as he asked. In her room, she lay down, but sleep didn't come.

Would she ever be able to close her eyes without wondering who was watching her?

Lying beneath the coverlet, she listened to the sounds of the night. About an hour later, she heard Wyatt and Patrick talking quietly in the living room. Wyatt must be taking over the watch.

How would she ever be able to thank him and Barb for their kindness?

As the night wore on, she eventually dozed, but woke again when she heard the sound of a truck approaching the cabin. It was barely light outside.

Jumping out of bed, she hurried into the living room. Wyatt was already on the porch with Patrick at his side. Shelby watched through the window as one of the sheriff department's white SUVs pulled to a stop in front of the house.

Two men got out. Both had their hands on the butts of their guns.

The driver stepped forward and Shelby recognized Sheriff Reed.

"Patrick Rivers, step out with your hands where I can see them."

Shelby raced to the door and yanked it open. "What's going on?"

"Stay back, Miss Mason." Deputy Olson moved to stand beside the sheriff.

Patrick sent Shelby a look plainly asking her to stay put. He walked down the steps toward the two men with his hands up. "What's this about?"

Deputy Olson stepped forward and quickly twisted Patrick's arms behind his back. "Patrick Rivers, you're under arrest for assault and rape."

SEVENTEEN

This can't be happening. Not again.

Bile rose in Patrick's throat. For a second, he thought he was going to be sick all over Deputy Olson's khaki uniform.

With no regard for his comfort, his arms were pulled behind him. Cold steel encircled his wrists.

"You have the right to remain silent. If you give up that right…"

The deputy's voice droned on. Patrick's eyes locked with Shelby's. "I didn't do it."

She didn't say a word. She simply stood there with a stunned expression on her face.

Barb walked out onto the porch with the boys at her side. Wyatt sent her back inside with a quick word.

Sheriff Reed bellied up to Patrick. "Y'all got away with rape once, but this time I'm locking you up for good. You shoulda stayed gone."

Wyatt stepped forward. "When and where did this alleged rape take place?"

"Covington. Last night."

Shelby darted down the steps to stand beside Patrick. "Then he couldn't have done it. He was here. He has an alibi."

"That's right, Sheriff," Wyatt added.

Fixing his scowl on Shelby, Reed said, "All night? You can swear that he never left? I'm asking for the whole truth, Miss Mason."

Wringing her hands, Shelby said, "He was outside for a while, but he didn't leave."

"Outside for how long, miss?"

"I don't know."

"Ten minutes? Thirty minutes?"

She pressed her hand to her lips. Her fingers were trembling. "I don't know, but I would have heard the truck or his bike engine if he'd gone anywhere. I barely slept last night."

Patrick stayed silent. He knew how useless it was to argue with the law.

Olson shoved Patrick toward the vehicle. "He could have pushed the bike and started it away from the house where you wouldn't hear it."

Shelby raked a hand through her tangled hair. "Then there would be tracks in the mud."

She ran to the road, searching the ground, then spun around and held out her hands. "There aren't any tire marks except yours."

Reed motioned to his deputy, who opened the door to the back seat. "The rain coulda washed them away. The woman identified him by name and even gave us a description of his bike. Said he took her for a spin on it first. It's a one-of-a-kind, ain't it, Rivers?"

The story was absurd. Patrick stared at the sheriff in disbelief. "Why would I be stupid enough to give this woman my real name and a ride on my bike?"

"'Cause you didn't think she'd talk. Guess the money you gave her to keep quiet wasn't enough." Olson put his hand on Patrick's head to guide him in.

Patrick shook him off and looked at Wyatt. "Take care of Shelby. Get her out of town."

Wyatt nodded but didn't speak.

Did his friend think he was guilty this time, too?

Olson forced Patrick's head down, and he entered the police car without further protest. As the door slammed shut, he focused his gaze on Shelby.

She looked so frantic. He wanted to tell her it was okay, but he knew it wouldn't be. Someone had gone to a lot of trouble to get him out of the way.

As the sheriff's vehicle pulled away, Shelby rounded on Wyatt. "Don't even think about it. I am not leaving town while Patrick sits in jail for something he didn't do. We have to help him."

"I can't help him. Not this time." His voice held such an odd quality.

Shelby looked at him closely. "What do you mean, *this time?*"

"Ten years ago, I was there. I followed Coral and Patrick. I saw them together. It wasn't rape."

Shelby couldn't begin to sort out the jumbled emotions and thoughts running through her mind. "Then why didn't you say something when he was arrested?"

He glanced at the door of the cabin. "I wanted him to suffer for having the woman I loved—or thought I loved. I didn't know what real love was until I met Barb. By then it was too late."

"Oh, Wyatt."

Laying a hand on his shoulder, Shelby offered him what comfort she could. "Maybe you didn't come forward ten years ago, but we can't change that. We have to prove Patrick is innocent now."

"How?"

"We'll think of something. Why didn't we hear the bike being ridden away?"

"I did hear an engine last night."

Shelby bit her lip. She had, too. She'd seen Patrick come in soaking wet when it was only sprinkling at the time.

Had he been soaked from riding through the rain on his way back from Covington?

No. He wasn't guilty.

She loved him, and she was going to prove he was innocent.

The sound of another vehicle making its way down the road drew their attention. A gray van pulled to a stop in the yard. It had FBI Crime Scene written in bold letters along the side.

Wyatt let out a low whistle. "Reed has called in some help. He must really want to make sure these charges stick."

A woman stepped out of the driver's side, and Shelby recognized FBI agent Jodie Gilmore.

Shelby's spirits lifted. "That's the best thing he could have possibly done for Patrick."

She hurried toward Jodie. "He didn't do it."

Jodie's smile was guarded and tinged with sympathy. "I know he's a friend of yours."

Wyatt came up to stand beside Shelby. "What's the FBI doing investigating a local rape case?"

"A report has come to light that leads us to believe this case may be connected to the murders."

Shelby frowned. "What kind of report?"

"I'm not at liberty to discuss that."

Thinking back, Shelby saw the faces of the deputies when she told them about the short red hairs in her missing Bible and their accusations that Patrick was always on hand when she had been threatened.

Shaking her head, she said, "Sheriff Reed can't possibly think Patrick had anything to do with the murders. He wasn't even here then."

"Agent Pierce did a little checking. Mr. Rivers wasn't in L.A. at the time of either murder. In fact, his whereabouts during the end of December and all of January are unknown."

Shelby couldn't believe what she was hearing. "What motive would Patrick have for killing Dylan or Earl?"

"Dylan's sister, Ava, was the one who reported him for rape. Maybe killing Dylan was his way of getting revenge. We haven't uncovered a connection to Earl Farley, but we're still looking."

Shelby ran a hand through her hair. "Patrick wasn't in L.A. because he was traveling through Mexico on vacation. Ask his boss."

"We're checking into that."

"Patrick doesn't have red hair! There were red hairs found at the scene of both Earl and Dylan's murders."

"How did you know that?" Jodie demanded.

"Wendy's brother-in-law works for the police department. Jocelyn has breakfast with me once a week. The murders are practically all this town talks about. Patrick doesn't have red hair, and little Sarah isn't afraid of him. He didn't rape or murder anyone."

"The hairs were from a human-hair wig, which he could easily have purchased."

"I don't care if you show me a sales receipt for a dozen wigs with his name on them. I know he didn't do it."

"Shelby, I'm going to ask you and the Tibbs family to stay inside while our crime scene techs do their work."

"They need to check the bike for fingerprints," Shelby declared, starting for the building at the side of the house. A man in a gray jumpsuit carrying a large black case was already headed in that direction.

Jodie grabbed Shelby by the arm and pulled her to a stop. "Let us do our job."

"If someone pushed the cycle away from the shed and rode it into Covington, there should be fingerprints or DNA or something on the bike that doesn't belong to Patrick."

Please, Lord, let them prove he didn't do this.

The crime scene tech was already stretching yellow crime scene tape across the front of the shed.

Wyatt shoved his hands in his pockets. A deep scowl creased his forehead. "That road gets as slimy as a gator's belly when it rains. A man would have a hard time pushing Patrick's big cycle far enough away for us not to hear it start. And then push it back in here? He'd be one strong dude. The bike should be covered in mud if it was moved."

Jodie steered Shelby back toward the cabin. "I'll listen to what you have to say, but let's go inside."

Shelby nodded and started to turn away when she saw the man in the shed kneel beside the bike to examine the ground. He withdrew a swab from his kit.

"That's it." Shelby looked at Wyatt. "Tell Barb to bring her camera out here right now. We may have proof the bike hasn't been moved since yesterday morning."

"You're right." He took off at a run.

Turning to the crime scene technician, Shelby took a step toward him and called out, "Sir, don't touch that oil spill."

He paused with his swab a few inches from it. He glanced at Jodie. Shelby saw them exchange looks.

She quickly explained. "You don't understand. Patrick parked his motorcycle in there the night we arrived. Monday night."

Jodie frowned. "So?"

"Patrick said his bike has a…a…a cracked gasket. It was leaking oil. There was a big puddle of it between the tires yesterday morning."

Barb came running up with her camera and handed it to Shelby. Quickly, Shelby scrolled through the images until she found the one of Mark making a face at the oil on his finger. The glint of the puddle in front of him reflected the light through the open doorway.

Shelby handed the camera to Jodie. "See the puddle? There's no way the bike could have been moved without leaving oily tire tracks all the way to the door. There's a date stamp and time on all these pictures. They were taken yesterday morning."

Jodie walked over to the shed. The ground in front of the door was muddy, but the area just inside was dry. "I'd say that motorcycle is at least five feet from this doorway, wouldn't you, Ed?"

Her coworker nodded. "About that."

"Are there tire tracks or footprints in that oil between the tires?"

"No, ma'am."

"Could you get that cycle out of there without going through the oil?"

"I'm guessing the bike weighs six to seven hundred pounds. I don't see how."

Jodie studied the picture. Stepping to one side, she focused the camera and took a picture. Holding it for the tech to look at, she asked, "Does that look like the same size and shape of puddle to you?"

He studied both pictures, then nodded. "It does."

Grinning, Shelby hugged Barb, then spun to face Jodie. "If the woman who accused him said he took her for a ride on his bike, she was lying."

Jodie nodded. "If she lied about that, then we need to find out what else she was lying about."

Inside the Loomis police station, Patrick sat on a bare cot inside a holding cell. The room stank of pungent pine cleaner and vomit. A weak fluorescent fixture on the stained ceiling outside the cell was the only source of light. He had no idea what time it was, but he figured he'd been there for hours. They'd taken his watch, his belt and the laces from his shoes when they booked him.

At least his trip to the interrogation room this time around had been mercifully shorter than his last visit.

Ten years ago he'd been a stunned kid barely twenty-two years old, who thought being innocent of a crime meant the sheriff would listen to what you had to say and let you go. Instead, he'd spent twelve hours being interrogated and brow-beaten to the point that he'd nearly confessed to something he hadn't done.

This time the only words out of his mouth had been, "I want a lawyer."

Since then, he'd been sitting inside this cell, worrying about Shelby's safety and waiting for his court-appointed attorney to show up.

Had Wyatt managed to get Shelby somewhere safe?

Patrick rubbed his hands across his face. Did she think he was guilty?

He'd seen the doubt in her eyes. He could bear almost anything accept knowing she thought he was capable of such a crime.

Leaning forward and propping his elbows on his knees, Patrick bowed his head.

Please, God, I don't care what happens to me. Just keep Shelby safe. And, God, thank You for the blessing of Shelby—and for a renewed relationship with You.

The sound of footsteps signaled the approach of someone coming down the hall. Maybe his attorney was finally here. Patrick rose to his feet.

It wasn't a lawyer. Sheriff Reed stopped in front of the cell.

With a fierce scowl on his face, the sheriff unlocked the door and pulled it open. "You're free to go, Rivers."

Eyeing the man in disbelief, Patrick didn't move. "Why?"

"Your alibi checks out—for now."

Relief shot through Patrick's body. He blinked hard and took a deep breath. Was this real?

Sheriff Reed stepped aside. "Don't leave town."

Patrick sent up a quick prayer of thanks and walked out the door.

"First, you tell me to leave, then you want me to stay. I wish you'd make up your mind, Sheriff."

Patrick smiled as he heard the sheriff muttering behind him.

Just outside the holding cell area, he collected his things from a freckle-faced young sergeant at the booking desk. After threading his belt through the loops in his jeans and buckling it, Patrick sat down to lace his shoes.

"Mr. Rivers, I'm Federal Agent Gilmore." A woman with blond hair approached him.

Great. Now the FBI wanted him. He tipped his head to look at her. "Can I finish tying my shoes or should I turn my laces in again?"

A slight smile curved her delicate lips. "I'm not here to arrest you. I'm the one who got you out."

"Then you have my eternal thanks."

"Just doing my job. After Shelby Mason convinced me your bike hadn't been moved, we knew your accuser was lying. I went to have a little chat with her."

"Who is she?"

"I'm sorry, I can't give you that information."

"I need to talk to her. I need to find out who put her up to this."

"We're checking a few leads, but unfortunately it appears

she has already left town. Fortunately, her neighbor was very helpful."

"How so?"

"He was taking out his trash, and he saw the woman in question getting into a dark sedan at the same time she stated she was being raped by you outside a bar in Covington."

"So we don't know who she was with? Did he get a license number or anything?"

"No. According to him, she's a party girl and seeing her get in a strange car wasn't all that unusual."

Jodie nodded toward the door leading to the waiting area. "I thought I might warn you that there's quite a media circus going on out there."

Puzzled, he asked, "Why?"

Shooting a sour glance at the officer behind the desk, she said, "Apparently, this department has a leak that makes the Mississippi River look like a drainage ditch. I believe the term *serial rapist* is being bandied about by the press. The news is all over town."

"Thanks for the warning."

"Can you prove you were traveling in Mexico last December and January?"

Puzzled, he asked, "Why?"

"Just answer the question."

He considered refusing, but thought better of it. "My passport is in my safe deposit box in L.A. It was stamped when I left and reentered the country. I can give you the names of some hotels where I stayed. I paid cash, but I ride a unique bike. Someone might remember me."

"All right, write them down for me." She handed him a pen and paper. After jotting down the names, he handed the sheet back.

She looked them over and nodded. "You should also know that Shelby Mason is waiting outside."

"She is?" He shot to his feet, happiness flooding his heart.

Agent Gilmore laid a hand on his shoulder. "She's a good friend to have in your corner. If she believes in someone, she never gives up."

"Did you know she's been receiving threats?"

"We'll be keeping a closer eye on her. If you'll excuse me, I have to confer with a colleague."

She left and Patrick braced himself to face the wolf pack waiting for him outside. This time, he wouldn't head out of town with his tail between his legs. He had a voice and he'd speak up for himself.

Pulling open the door, he saw a group of reporters and several news crews clustered around a couple standing across the room. Coral Travis was hanging on the arm of her fiancé, councilman Wendell Bixby, as he addressed the group.

"Loomis is a much safer town tonight, ladies and gentleman. A miscarriage of justice had gone on for ten years, but now my future wife can rest easy. Patrick Rivers is behind bars where he belongs."

Patrick squared his shoulders and walked forward. "You should get your facts straight, Councilman. I'm a free man. In fact, the only miscarriage of justice here is the slur on my good name."

Like a flock of birds, the reporters swooped to Patrick's side of the room. Bright lights shone in his face and people began shouting questions at him. Finally, he held up his hand.

"Ten years ago I was accused of drugging and raping Coral Travis. None of that is true. The charges against me were dropped for lack of evidence, but that didn't clear my name."

Patrick paused, wondering how to put into words everything raging in his soul. As he did, he caught sight of Shelby.

In the corner of the room, she stood with her hands clasped

beneath her chin, trying to be invisible again. The look shining in her eyes made his heart swell with pride. He held out his hand.

Straightening her shoulders, she crossed the room and linked her fingers with his. If they weren't surrounded by people, he would have kissed her.

Glancing over her head, he saw a look of hatred cross Coral's face. The threats had to stop. Everything had to come out in the open.

The outside doors to the room opened. Ava and Max entered. Agent Gilmore hadn't been kidding when she said the news was all over town. A second later, Wyatt and Barb came in behind them.

Patrick gave his attention back to the reporters. This was his one chance to clear his name.

"I was accused of using a date-rape drug. I barely knew what they were ten years ago, but I've done my research. Drugs like GHB, Rohypnol and Ketamine often have no color, smell or taste and can easily be added to drinks without a victim's knowledge. They take effect quickly. The victim can suffer nausea, vomiting, hallucinations and lost time. They have distorted perceptions of sight and sound, even out-of-body experiences."

Coral shook off the hand of her fiancé and stormed across the room. "I suffered all of those things. You slipped something in my drink, and the next thing I knew I was being assaulted by you."

"You didn't let me finish, Coral. A hallmark of these drugs is that the victim can remain unconscious for up to twelve hours. How long after we left the party were we discovered in bed together?"

"I don't know. I don't remember."

"One hour. Your roommate found us one hour after we left

the party. You didn't have trouble walking or talking or re-counting what had happened. I just want to know why you lied. Why you let the police haul me away in handcuffs."

Wendell reached her side and said, "Coral, let's leave."

"No. He belongs in jail and everyone should know it."

"Patrick doesn't belong in jail, Coral. I was there, and I know the truth." Wyatt left his wife's side and came to stand next to Patrick.

Puzzled by Wyatt's comment, Patrick said, "What do you mean?"

Wyatt glanced toward his wife. She nodded slightly. "Shelby said she overheard Coral talking to someone," he continued. "That someone was me. I'd finally gotten up the courage to ask Coral out."

He fastened his gaze on her. "Do you remember what you said? You said you wouldn't waste your time on a second string player like me. Then you left with him."

"You were second string and you still are. Look how you turned out. A mill worker," Coral scoffed.

"I am a mill worker with a loving wife and two beautiful boys. They're much more than I deserve. I'm sorry, Patrick. I followed the two of you when you left the party. When you went into Coral's dorm room, I crept up to the window. I saw everything."

The shock of his friend's betrayal rocked Patrick to the core. "Why didn't you say something to clear me?"

"I hated you that night for having everything I could never have. For being everything I could never be."

"But to leave me in jail?"

"I regretted keeping quiet, but I didn't know how to undo it. I avoided you after that because I felt so guilty each time I looked at your face. I was glad you left town, but not as glad as I am that you've come back. I hope in time you can forgive me."

Walking away, Wyatt draped his arm around his wife's shoulders and they left together.

A reporter asked, "Mr. Rivers, what about today's rape charges? Were they also dropped for lack of evidence?"

"No." Shelby spoke up for the first time. "Patrick has an alibi. His accuser lied. We don't know why, but we think she was paid to do so. Care to comment about that, Coral?"

"I had nothing to do with it. Wendell, please take me home."

She brushed past the media but was stopped by Ava. "Coral, you made me party to a terrible lie. Why?"

"I thought he was going to be *somebody*. Instead, he tells me he doesn't want to play professional football. He wants to build motorcycles. Then you walked in. Honestly, what was I supposed to say, Ava? I didn't want a Renault to think I'd sleep with a grease monkey."

Tossing her head back, Coral walked out, leaving her bewildered-looking fiancé behind her.

He swallowed hard as he looked at Max. "Mr. Pershing, I had no idea."

"Don't worry, Wendell, I'm not withdrawing my support of your campaign."

"Thank you, sir."

"As long as the deed for Mr. Rivers's property shows up by tomorrow."

"It will. I'll see to it."

Patrick's head was awhirl with everything he'd learned. It was almost more than he could take in. He needed balance—he needed Shelby.

He looked around, but she was gone.

EIGHTEEN

Shelby sank onto a chair at side of the waiting room. Most of the reporters were trickling out, and she needed time to gather her thoughts.

Memory after memory surfaced in her mind like so many bubbles rising to the top of a shaken soda bottle. They fizzed and splattered against her brain, making her wonder if they were real events or only something she had dreamed.

"Is this seat taken?" Patrick stood in front of her looking wonderfully handsome and as dazed as she felt.

She patted the chair. "I'm sorry about Wyatt."

Patrick sank down beside her. "It took a lot of guts for him to come forward. I think things will get better for us both."

"I pray they will."

"I understand that I owe my freedom to you. That you proved my bike never left Wyatt's shed."

"Agent Gilmore would have figured it out in about five more minutes. I just rushed it."

"Thanks." Patrick took her hand and raised it to his lips. The simple gesture melted her heart.

He said, "Why don't I take you home? It's been a long day."

Shelby pressed a hand to her forehead. "I'd love to go home, but I can't. I need to talk to Agent Gilmore."

"About what?"

"When you started listing the effects of the date-rape drugs, I knew it had happened to me."

His face registered shock, quickly followed by compassion. "Darling, I'm so sorry."

"I wasn't raped. At least I don't think so, but I believe I was drugged. I remember feeling so sick. I don't know why I didn't think of it sooner. It just never clicked. I thought it was a dream. A dream that wouldn't go away."

"When did this happen?"

"Four years ago at a Christmas party. I think Dylan raped Leah that night."

The police interrogation room was small and cramped with gray cinder block walls that left Shelby feeling chilly. The wooden chair she perched on offered nothing in the way of comfort.

The door opened suddenly, and Agent Sam Pierce walked in. He was the kind of man who commanded attention. He was a man used to being in charge.

He took a seat on the edge of the table, looming over her. "What new evidence do you have about Dylan Renault's murder?"

Jodie would have been much less intimidating. Shelby bit her lip. "It isn't evidence, exactly."

She wished the police had let Patrick stay with her. Sam had interviewed her several times following Leah's disappearance. When he was working, he was intimidating to say the least.

"Shelby, I know you're a friend of my wife, but that doesn't mean you can waste the FBI's time."

"I'm not!" She took a breath and forged ahead. "Four years ago, Leah worked for Dylan Renault."

"We know that."

"That year, Leah convinced me to go to the company Christmas party with her. She was uncomfortable being in a social setting with Dylan. She wanted me to come along for moral support and to run interference."

"He was known as a ladies' man."

"Dylan wouldn't leave Leah alone at the party. We were getting ready to leave, and I remember he brought us cups of punch. He insisted we have a Christmas toast with him. That's when things started to get strange. Leah said she felt sick and within a matter of minutes, so did I."

"How much had you had to drink?"

"Well, that's just it. We weren't drinking alcohol. All we'd had was ginger ale until the punch."

"Are you suggesting someone spiked your drinks?"

"Yes. We both got sick very quickly. The room was spinning like crazy. Someone helped me to a sofa in another room. That's the last thing I remember. When I woke up in the morning, the party was over and Leah was gone."

"Gone?"

"A maid told me Dylan had taken her home because she wasn't feeling well. I couldn't believe she just left me there. When I got to her apartment, I knew something was wrong."

"What do you mean?"

"I don't know how to describe it, but I knew she was keeping something from me. She wouldn't look at me. She said we must have had some kind of twenty-four-hour flu bug. I *felt* like I had the flu, but I noticed bruises on her wrists and on her face. The next day, she quit her job. I think Dylan Renault drugged her and raped her."

"So she took her revenge by killing him. Did you help her?"

Aghast, Shelby stared at him in astonishment. "No, of course not!"

"So she killed him on her own."

"No! What are you trying to do?"

"Your story provides a very strong motive for murder."

Shelby stared at him open-mouthed. "Leah didn't kill anyone."

"Did Earl Farley find out the child wasn't his? I can understand how he must have felt. Angry. Betrayed. Perhaps Leah was defending herself. Earl was known to have a temper."

Shelby held up both hands. "No. No. No. Leah did not kill Earl. She did not kill Dylan. Why are you saying these things?"

"I'm trying to get to the bottom of three murders."

How could she make him understand? "Leah is missing. She's a victim."

"With a friend who would do anything for her, even help cover her tracks."

A cold calm settled over Shelby. Sam was trying to do his job, but he had it all wrong. "Am I under arrest?"

"Not at this point."

"Then I'm leaving. I told you what I suspect and that's all I have to say."

"Don't go far, Miss Mason. We may have more questions for you."

Rising on shaky legs, Shelby made her way out of the room.

Patrick was waiting outside when Shelby finally walked out of the police station. He took one look at her face and rushed to her. "Hey, what's the matter? You look like you're about to keel over."

"I need you to hold me."

"Of course." He wrapped his arms around her. The feel of

her small, trembling body nestled against his brought out every protective instinct he possessed. "Was there another threat? Did someone try to hurt you?"

"No."

She looked up at him with wide frightened eyes. "I told Sam Pierce what I suspected. He said it gives Leah a motive to have killed her husband and Dylan. He thinks I helped her."

"What? That's crazy."

"I should have kept quiet. I never should have said anything."

"Shelby, you were right to try to help."

"It doesn't feel right."

"What feels right is holding you. A few hours ago I thought I might never do this." He gently kissed her upturned face.

"I love you, Shelby," he murmured against her cheek.

She tightened her grip around him. "I love you more. I thank God for you. With you and my faith back, I know we can make it. I believe that with all my heart, Patrick."

"The sheriff told me I can't leave town."

"Really?" She leaned back to gaze up at him. "The FBI told me the same thing. It sounds like we could be spending a lot of time together."

"Sounds perfect."

"What about your friends in California?"

He shrugged. "They'll understand when I tell them I've found the woman of my dreams. Someone quite smart suggested I start my own custom cycle shop. What do you think of that idea?"

Smiling, she tipped her head. "I think it sounds perfect."

It *was* a good idea, but he wouldn't be able to do it by himself. He'd need a partner. Someone familiar with the area to help him get started. Would Wyatt be interested? The thought of working with his friend again made him smile.

Shelby pressed her face to his chest once more. "We have one more place to go tonight."

"Where is that?"

Sighing, she said, "I have to talk to Leah's brother."

NINETEEN

Shelby paused outside Clint's front door. Looking over her shoulder at Patrick, she asked, "What am I doing? What do I really know?"

He laid a comforting hand on her shoulder. "You had to tell the truth."

"Some help that was. All I did was give the authorities a stronger motive to suspect Leah killed Dylan—and that I helped her."

"If Dylan is Sarah's father, it's going to change a lot of things for that little girl."

"I know. It's just that Clint has suffered so much already. Now I'm going to pour salt in his wounds."

"It'll be hard for him to hear, but it will be better coming from you. You're Leah's friend."

"I pray you're right." Biting her lip, Shelby pressed the doorbell and waited.

After a few moments, Clint opened the door. A puzzled frown creased his forehead. "Shelby, what are you doing here?"

"I need to talk to you. It's about Leah."

Hope brightened his eyes. "Have you heard something?"

"Not about her disappearance. This has to do with Sarah. May we come in?"

"Of course." His disappointment was obvious and wounded Shelby's heart. Taking a step back, he gestured for them to enter.

Clint lived in an old, two-story home that faced the park. As a contractor himself, he had done much of the work re-modeling and updating it. The clack of Shelby's heels sounded unnaturally loud on the hardwood floors. She was relieved when they reached the living room where carpet muffled the noise.

His home was clean and neat except for a few of Sarah's toys left lying about. Clearly a bachelor's place, the room con-tained cushy chairs, a sofa and a TV. The beautiful framed wa-tercolors of the bayou on his walls sent a shiver over Shelby's skin. Leah's body might be out there somewhere.

Shelby sat on the sofa, glad to have Patrick at her side. She reached for his hand and squeezed it. His presence brought her consolation and strength.

Please, Lord, let this be the right thing to do.

Clint sat in the chair opposite them. "What'd y'all want to tell me about Sarah?"

Taking a deep breath, Shelby gently began her story. When she was finished, she waited for Clint to speak.

"No!" He shook his head, denial etched deep in his features.

Shooting to his feet, he began pacing across the room. "She would have told me if Dylan had…done something like that."

"I was so confused when the drug wore off that I wasn't certain about anything—where I was, what had happened. She may not have wanted to admit it, even to herself."

He rounded on her. "See, you're not sure."

"I'm sorry, Clint. I know this is difficult. If I had solid evidence it would be easier, but all I have is my gut instinct.

Her mouth was bruised. She had bruises on her wrists. She quit her job the next day. She never talked about that night. She married Earl almost right away. Sarah was born in September. Nine months later."

Clint sank onto the chair and dropped his head in his hands. "I don't know what to believe.

"She would have told me," he repeated, almost to himself.

Leaning forward, Shelby tried to make him understand what it had been like. "Afterward, I had these dreams about a man standing over me, laughing at me, making me feel stupid and dirty. I wanted to block it all out of my head. I didn't think it was real. I can't imagine what it must have been like for Leah if she was raped."

"Dear God, don't let it be true." Clint cupped his hand over his mouth and blinked back tears.

Gently, Shelby added, "In light of Dylan's last words, it makes sense."

Patrick spoke up for the first time. "There's something else you should know, Clint. The police and the FBI are looking at this information as motive."

Clint frowned. "Motive? For what?"

"They say this gives Leah a reason to have killed Dylan and disappeared on purpose."

Clint rose to his feet and crossed to the window to stare out into the darkness. "No. Even if these speculations are true, Leah wouldn't hurt anyone."

Shelby exchanged a pointed glance with Patrick. He nodded. Rising, she crossed to Clint's side and laid a hand on his shoulder. "There's only one way to discover the truth. Give permission for the FBI to test Sarah's DNA."

After a long silence, he turned to face her. "I'm not going to do that."

Shelby nodded in understanding.

"Why not?" Patrick demanded.

Glancing at him, Clint's lips twisted into a sad half smile. "Because it would be the same as saying I believe my sister is a liar."

As they left Clint's house, Shelby welcomed Patrick's arm around her shoulder. "Maybe Clint is right. Maybe Dylan didn't assault Leah."

If only she believed it, but in her heart she knew differently.

"He should allow DNA testing." Patrick shortened his steps to match hers.

They stopped by unspoken consent at her car. She said, "Everything that has happened in Loomis is somehow related to Leah. We're missing something."

"There are a lot of people working on this, Shelby, but sometimes these things are never solved."

"I have to prepare myself for that, don't I?"

A car came down the street, and Shelby turned her face away from the bright lights. As she did, she caught a glimpse of a face peering out of the shrubbery in front of Clint's window.

Disbelief held Shelby motionless until the car passed by. She grabbed Patrick's arm. "It can't be."

"What?" He looked around quickly.

"I saw her. I saw Leah!"

The figure near the house moved away. Shelby started after her and screamed, "Leah, wait! Leah, stop!"

To Shelby's amazement, her friend began running. As Leah crossed the drive of the house next door, motion-sensing lights lit up the darkness.

Shelby had one clear look at her face when Leah glanced over her shoulder. Without slowing, she ran across the street and into the park.

Shelby followed, screaming Leah's name until she lost sight of her in the darkness.

Patrick caught up with Shelby as she stood at the edge of the park yelling at the top of her lungs. He grasped her shoulders. "Shelby, what are you doing?"

She didn't take her eyes off the park. "I saw her. Why would she run from me?"

Lights came on at a few more houses as people stepped out to see what was going on. Clint was among them. He came jogging toward them.

"What happened?"

Shelby whirled to face him. "I saw Leah."

"What? Where?" Clint moved to scan the park.

"She was outside your window looking in. When I called her name, she started running. Clint, why would she run away?"

Patrick pulled Shelby close. She was on the verge of hysterics.

"Are you sure it was Leah?" Clint's voice vibrated with uncertainty and hope.

A small crowd had begun to gather on the sidewalk. Shelby pressed a hand to her forehead. "Yes. Her hair was different. Short and dyed a dark color."

"Then maybe it wasn't her."

Shelby managed to calm herself enough to answer. "I know it was Leah. I know it was."

She looked at Clint. "What is she hiding from?"

EPILOGUE

Two days later, the killer paced back and forth across a small room. Fury boiled beneath the surface, threatening to explode into scathing violence. All because Shelby Mason couldn't keep her fat mouth shut.

Toying with her, scaring the miserable little mouse had been fun, but useless in the end.

Killing her outright would have been better. Only Patrick Rivers's arrival had saved her.

It was too late to do anything about it now. Both the FBI and that fool Rivers were watching Shelby like hawks. The ploy to get rid of her ardent protector had failed, too.

Failure was not an option! Not acceptable!

Covering all the tracks of that unsuccessful gambit had taken a nasty bit of clean-up work. The greedy little liar hired for her acting ability was spending her hard-earned money at the bottom of the swamp.

That was one body that would never resurface.

Unlike Leah Farley.

The gossip was all over town that Shelby had seen her friend outside Clint Herald's place. If it had been Leah, why had she vanished again without speaking to anyone?

Was she smarter than she looked?

Calming down, the killer laid a red wig and gun into the small secret hiding place at the back of the closet. Stroking the soft hair of the wig, the killer smiled.

"Don't worry. You won't be in here long. You'll both be needed again very soon—if Leah Farley really is alive."

* * * * *

Dear Reader

I hope you are enjoying all the books in the WITHOUT A TRACE series. *A Cloud of Suspicion* was my first suspense novel and in some ways my most difficult book to date. Writing a story inside the continuity proved to be a challenge. I couldn't have done it without the help of the other authors in this series. Each and every one of them helped me in countless ways. Those talented ladies have my special thanks.

For me, the toughest thing was crafting a story where the murderer isn't revealed. Although I already know "who done it," I can't wait to read the final books in this series. The twists just keep coming.

I've learned a thing or two while working on *A Cloud of Suspicion*. For one, I learned I like to write scary stuff. My next book for Love Inspired Suspense, *Speed Trap,* will be out in September of 2009.

I'd love to hear what you think of the series. You can e-mail me at pat@patriciadavids.com or write me at P.O. Box 16714, Wichita, Kansas 67216.

Blessings to all,

Patricia Davids

QUESTIONS FOR DISCUSSION

1. Did you enjoy *A Cloud of Suspicion*? Why or why not?

2. Did you think Shelby Mason was an unlikely heroine? Why?

3. What personality trait or traits did Shelby need to overcome to become a stronger woman?

4. What was your impression of Patrick Rivers when he first appeared? Did your impression change after finishing the book?

5. Did you find his character well-drawn or superficial?

6. Loomis is a town rife with gossip. Do you feel it accurately portrays small town life?

7. Have the authors of the WITHOUT A TRACE books done a good job of keeping the recurring characters true to form?

8. Did the setting of the story appeal to you? Why or why not?

9. Shelby's faith was strong from start to finish, but Patrick had to begin a journey back to God. Do you know someone who lost their faith and then rediscovered it?

10. As a young man, Patrick was accused of a crime he didn't commit. Was he wrong to leave town or should he have

stayed and faced down the gossip? What would you have done in his place?

11. Motorcycles have a special appeal and can evoke strong emotions. Do you associate them with fun and freedom or a lack of responsibility? Why?

12. Wyatt allowed jealousy to ruin his best friend's life. When has jealousy adversely affected your life or the life of someone you know?

Turn the page for an exciting sneak preview of
DEADLY COMPETITION
by Roxanne Rustand,
the next title in the
WITHOUT A TRACE *series,*
available next month.

ONE

Mandy Erick flinched as the door of the Greyhound slid shut behind her.

The bus lumbered away, taking with it her chance to reach Texas or California or Oregon anytime soon. Leaving her standing on the edge of Loomis, Louisiana: a backwater town in the middle of nowhere.

Though maybe the middle of nowhere was the safest place for someone who'd had to leave her old identity behind.

A cold late April rain dripped off her hair and onto the collar of her thin jacket, and she wished she'd had time to pack an umbrella. A raincoat. For that matter, an extra pair of shoes.

But lingering could've meant being discovered. Being stopped before she could leave town. A few minor possessions were a small price to pay for her life.

The lone waitress came back to the booth in the corner every ten minutes or so, offering more coffee. Probably wishing Mandy would finally leave, since she'd finished her egg-and-one-piece-of-toast breakfast well over an hour ago.

But where did one go in a town like this at seven in the morning—and in the rain?

"More coffee?" The waitress, skinny and weathered, looked as if she'd been left out in the elements for a few years to cure, but there was a warmer hint of concern in her voice this time around.

She stood at Mandy's elbow with a coffeepot in one hand, her other hand on her hip, then snagged an upended cup from a neighboring table, filled it, and slid into the opposite side of Mandy's booth. The faded badge on her yellow scrub top read NONNIE.

"Where're y'all headed?"

Mandy shifted in her seat and avoided the woman's knowing eyes. "West. I…have relatives out there."

"Gotta long ways to go." Nonnie took a long sip from her cup and then cradled it in her gnarled hands. "Lookin' to stay around for a while?"

"I—" Mandy glanced around the small diner, wondering if she dared ask about a job. Realizing at once that with the low base pay paid to most waitresses plus the minimal tips possible in a place like this, she wouldn't be able to afford rent, much less save money for her escape. "I don't know."

Nonnie seemed to read her mind. "Small place, I know. Me and my hubby own it, though. He cooks, I tend tables. We'll have a good little crowd of regulars starting around seven-thirty." She pulled a thin newspaper from her apron pocket and pushed it across the table. "I grabbed this from the back, just in case you're looking for a job or a place to stay."

Mandy ventured a quick glance at her, but found only genuine concern on the woman's face. "Thanks."

"You best be careful, though. There's been trouble 'round

here this spring. Pretty little gal like you oughta watch her step."

"T-trouble?"

"Three murders back in January, and a sweet young woman went missing, so maybe there was a fourth. All of that, yet there's some who still put way too much stock in frippery." She gave a snort of disgust and tapped the headline of the paper that read MOTHER OF THE YEAR PAGEANT IN FULL SWING! "Whoooeee—you'd think them gals were runnin' for President. And most of 'em wouldn't be *my* idea of a good momma. Fancy ways, careers—their golf club more important than the PTA. But you can bet money talks, and one of those rich gals will win. Happens every year."

"Murders?" Mandy's stomach tied itself into a queasy knot.

Mandy's unease grew, tightening its icy grip on her stomach. Danger was following her. Now she'd landed in a place where she'd need to be on her guard even more. "Were the murders related?"

"Probably, to my mind. Everyone in Loomis is connected some way or another. Roots run deep in a place like this— some tangled in secrets and dark ways you just don' wanna know, *cher*."

The waitress made a shooing motion with her hand. "Go on, check the classifieds. It's just our local paper, but you might find something. You can use our phone, if need be." She stood. "I'd best go pass a mop over this floor so it can dry before things get busy."

Mandy watched the woman scurry back to the kitchen, then took a deep breath as she pulled a pen from her backpack and started scanning the ads.

She had no money to continue on, and she needed to find a safe place where she'd be beyond Dean's reach. With a low-profile job and a cheap place to live for a month or so, she could build up her reserve of cash.

Whatever the local troubles were, she'd keep her distance from people here, avoid saying too much, and she'd be on her way as fast as possible.

And she'd never, ever be back.

* * * * *

*Turn the page for a sneak peek
of Shirlee McCoy's suspense-filled story,
THE DEFENDER'S DUTY
On sale in May 2009 from
Steeple Hill Love Inspired® Suspense.*

After weeks in intensive care, police officer Jude
Sinclair is finally recovering from the hit-and-run
accident that nearly cost him his life. But was it an
accident after all? Jude has his doubts—which get
stronger when he spots a familiar black car outside his
house: the same kind that accelerated before running
him down two months ago. Whoever wants him dead
hasn't given up, and anyone close to Jude is in danger.
Especially Lacey Carmichael, the stubborn, beautiful
home-care aide who refuses to leave his side, even if it
means following him into danger....

"We don't have time for an argument," Jude said. "Take a look outside. What do you see?"

Lacey looked and shrugged. "The parking lot."

"Can you see your car?"

"Sure. It's parked under the streetlight. Why?"

"See the car to its left?"

"Yeah. It's a black sedan." Her heart skipped a beat as she said the words, and she leaned closer to the glass. "You don't think that's the same car you saw at the house tonight, do you?"

"I don't know, but I'm going to find out."

Lacey scooped up the grilled-cheese sandwich and shoved it into the carryout bag. "Let's go."

He eyed her for a moment, his jaw set, his gaze hot. *"We're* not going anywhere. You are staying here. I am going to talk to the driver of that car."

"I think we've been down this road before and I'm pretty sure we both know where it leads."

"It leads to you getting fired. Stay put until I get back, or forget about having a place of your own for a month." He stood and limped away, not even giving Lacey a second glance as he crossed the room and headed into the diner's kitchen area.

Probably heading for a back door.

Lacey gave him a one-minute head start and then followed, the hair on the back of her neck standing on end and issuing a warning she couldn't ignore. Danger. It was somewhere close by again, and there was no way she was going to let Jude walk into it alone. If he fired her, so be it. As a matter of fact, if he fired her, it might be for the best. Jude wasn't the kind of client she was used to working for. Sure, there'd been other young men, but none of them had seemed quite as vital or alive as Jude. He didn't seem to need her, and Lacey didn't want to be where she wasn't needed. On the other hand, she'd felt absolutely certain moving to Lynchburg was what God wanted her to do.

"So, which is it, Lord? Right or wrong?" She whispered the words as she slipped into the diner's hot kitchen. A cook glared at her, but she ignored him. Until she knew for sure why God had brought her to Lynchburg, Lacey could only do what she'd been paid to do—make sure Jude was okay.

With that in mind, she crossed the room, heading for the exit and the client that she was sure was going to be a lot more trouble than she'd anticipated when she'd accepted the job.

Jude eased around the corner of the restaurant, the dark alleyway offering him perfect cover as he peered into the parking lot. The car he'd spotted through the window of the restaurant was still parked beside Lacey's. Black. Four door. Honda. It matched the one that had pulled up in front of his house, and the one that had run him down in New York.

He needed to get closer.

A soft sound came from behind him. A rustle of fabric. A sigh of breath. Spring rain and wildflowers carried on the cold night air. Lacey.

Of course.

"I told you that you were going to be fired if you didn't stay where you were."

"Do you know how many times someone has threatened to fire me?"

"Based on what I've seen so far, a lot."

"Some of my clients fire me ten or twenty times a day."

"Then I guess I've got a ways to go." Jude reached back and grabbed her hand, pulling her up beside him.

"Is the car still there?"

"Yeah."

"Let me see." She squeezed in closer, her hair brushing his chin as she jockeyed for a better position.

Jude pulled her up short. Her wrist was warm beneath his hand. For a moment he was back in the restaurant, Lacey's creamy skin peeking out from under her dark sweater, white scars crisscrossing the tender flesh. She'd shoved her sleeve down too quickly for him to get a good look, but the glimpse he'd gotten was enough. There was a lot more to Lacey than met the eye. A lot she hid behind a quick smile and a quicker wit. She'd been hurt before, and he wouldn't let it happen again. No way was he going to drag her into danger. Not now. Not tomorrow. Not ever. As soon as they got back to the house, he was going to do exactly what he'd threatened—fire her.

"It's not the car." She said it with such authority, Jude stepped from the shadows and took a closer look.

"Why do you say that?"

"The one back at the house had tinted glass. Really dark. With this one, you can see in the back window. Looks like there is a couple sitting in the front seats. Unless you've got two people after you, I don't think that's the same car."

She was right.

Of course she was.

Jude could see inside the car, see the couple in the front seats. If he'd been thinking with his head instead of acting on the anger that had been simmering in his gut for months, he would have seen those things long before now. "You'd make a good detective, Lacey."

"You think so? Maybe I should make a career change. Give up home-care aide for something more dangerous and exciting." She laughed as she pulled away from his hold and stepped out into the parking lot, but there was tension in her shoulders and in the air. As if she sensed the danger that had been stalking Jude, felt it as clearly as Jude did.

"I'm not sure being a detective is as dangerous or as exciting as people think. Most days it's a lot of running into brick walls. Backing up, trying a new direction." He spoke as he led Lacey across the parking lot, his body still humming with adrenaline.

"That sounds like life to me. Running into brick walls, backing up and trying new directions."

"True, but in my job the brick walls happen every other day. In life, they're usually not as frequent." He waited while she got into her car, then closed the door, glancing in the black sedan as he walked past. An elderly woman smiled and waved at him, and Jude waved back, still irritated with himself for the mistake he'd made.

Now that he was closer, it was obvious the two cars he'd seen weren't the same. The one at his place had been sleeker and a little more sporty. Which proved that when a person wanted to see something badly enough, he did.

"That wasn't much of a meal for you. Sorry to cut things short for a false alarm." He glanced at Lacey as he got into the Mustang, and was surprised that her hand was shaking as she shoved the key into the ignition.

He put a hand on her forearm. "Are you okay?"

"Fine."

"For someone who is fine, your hands sure are shaking hard."

"How about we chalk it up to fatigue?"

"How about you admit you were scared?"

"Were? I still am." She started the car, and Jude let his hand fall away from her arm.

"You don't have to be. We're safe. For now."

"It's the 'for now' part that's got me worried. Who's trying to kill you, Jude? Why?"

"If I had the answers to those questions, we wouldn't be sitting here talking about it."

"You don't even have a suspect?"

"Lacey, I've got a dozen suspects. More. Every wife who's ever watched me cart her husband off to jail. Every son who's ever seen me put handcuffs on his dad. Every family member or friend who's sat through a murder trial and watched his loved one get convicted because of the evidence I put together."

"Have you made a list?"

"I've made a hundred lists. None of them have done me any good. Until the person responsible comes calling again, I've got no evidence, no clues and no way to link anyone to the hit and run."

"Maybe he won't come calling again. Maybe the hit and run was an accident, and maybe the sedan we saw outside your house was just someone who got lost and ended up in the wrong place." She sounded like she really wanted to believe it. He should let her. That's what he'd done with his family. Let them believe the hit and run was a fluke thing that had happened and was over. He'd done it to keep them safe. He'd do the opposite to keep Lacey from getting hurt.

* * * * *

Will Jude manage to scare Lacey away,
or will he learn that the best way
to keep her safe is to keep her close…
for as long as they both shall live?
To find out, read
THE DEFENDER'S DUTY
by Shirlee McCoy
Available May 2009
from Love Inspired Suspense

REQUEST YOUR FREE BOOKS!

2 FREE RIVETING INSPIRATIONAL NOVELS
PLUS 2 FREE MYSTERY GIFTS

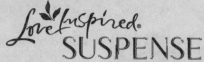

YES! Please send me 2 FREE Love Inspired® Suspense novels and my 2 FREE mystery gifts (gifts are worth about $10). After receiving them, if I don't wish to receive any more books, I can return the shipping statement marked "cancel". If I don't cancel, I will receive 4 brand-new novels every month and be billed just $4.24 per book in the U.S. or $4.74 per book in Canada, plus 25¢ shipping and handling per book and applicable taxes, if any*. That's a savings of over 20% off the cover price! I understand that accepting the 2 free books and gifts places me under no obligation to buy anything. I can always return a shipment and cancel at any time. Even if I never buy another book, the two free books and gifts are mine to keep forever.

123 IDN ERXX   323 IDN ERXM

Name	(PLEASE PRINT)	
Address		Apt. #
City	State/Prov.	Zip/Postal Code

Signature (if under 18, a parent or guardian must sign)

Order online at www.LoveInspiredSuspense.com
Or mail to Steeple Hill Reader Service:
IN U.S.A.: P.O. Box 1867, Buffalo, NY 14240-1867
IN CANADA: P.O. Box 609, Fort Erie, Ontario L2A 5X3

Not valid to current subscribers of Love Inspired Suspense books.

Want to try two free books from another series?
Call 1-800-873-8635 or visit www.morefreebooks.com

* Terms and prices subject to change without notice. N.Y. residents add applicable sales tax. Canadian residents will be charged applicable provincial taxes and GST. Offer not valid in Quebec. This offer is limited to one order per household. All orders subject to approval. Credit or debit balances in a customer's account(s) may be offset by any other outstanding balance owed by or to the customer. Please allow 4 to 6 weeks for delivery. Offer available while quantities last.

Your Privacy: Steeple Hill Books is committed to protecting your privacy. Our Privacy Policy is available online at www.SteepleHill.com or upon request from the Reader Service. From time to time we make our lists of customers available to reputable third parties who may have a product or service of interest to you. If you would prefer we not share your name and address, please check here. ☐